Dear Reader,

Looking back over [...] hard to
realize that twenty-six of them have gone by
since I wrote my first book—*Sister Peters in
Amsterdam.* It wasn't until I started writing about
her that I found that once I had started writing,
nothing was going to make me stop—and at
that time I had no intention of sending it to a
publisher. It was my daughter who urged me to
try my luck.

I shall never forget the thrill of having my first
book accepted—a thrill I still get each time a
new story is accepted. To me, writing is such a
pleasure, and seeing a story unfolding on my old
typewriter is like watching a film and wondering
how it will end. Happily, of course.

To have so many of my books republished is such
a delightful thing to happen and I can only hope
that those who read them will share my pleasure
in seeing them on the bookshelves again...and
enjoy reading them.

Betty Neels

Betty Neels spent her childhood and youth in Devonshire before training as a nurse and midwife. She was an army nursing sister during the war, married a Dutchman and subsequently lived in Holland for fourteen years. She lives with her husband in Dorset, and has a daughter and a grandson. Her hobbies are reading, animals, old buildings and writing. On retirement from nursing Betty started to write, incited by a lady in a library bemoaning the lack of romantic novels.

Mrs. Neels is always delighted to receive fan letters, but would truly appreciate it if they could be directed to Harlequin Mills & Boon Ltd., 18-24 Paradise Road, Richmond, Surrey, TW9 1SR, England.

Books by Betty Neels

HARLEQUIN ROMANCE

JUDITH	ENCHANTING SAMANTHA
MIDNIGHT SUN'S MAGIC	HEIDELBERG WEDDING
SUN AND CANDLELIGHT	POLLY
PHILOMENA'S MIRACLE	TULIPS FOR AUGUSTA
HANNAH	LAST APRIL FAIR
A MATTER OF CHANCE	TEMPESTUOUS APRIL
WINTER WEDDING	WHEN MAY FOLLOWS
STORMY SPRINGTIME	MIDSUMMER STAR

BETTY NEELS

LAST APRIL FAIR

COLLECTOR'S EDITION

HARLEQUIN®

TORONTO • NEW YORK • LONDON
AMSTERDAM • PARIS • SYDNEY • HAMBURG
STOCKHOLM • ATHENS • TOKYO • MILAN • MADRID
PRAGUE • WARSAW • BUDAPEST • AUCKLAND

ISBN 0-373-63135-9

LAST APRIL FAIR

First North American Publication 2000.

Copyright © 1980 by Betty Neels.

This edition published by arrangement with Harlequin Books S.A.

® and TM are trademarks of the publisher. Trademarks indicated with ® are registered in the United States Patent and Trademark Office, the Canadian Trade Marks Office and in other countries.

Visit us at www.eHarlequin.com

Printed in U.S.A.

CHAPTER ONE

MRS GREGSON'S elderly voice, raised in its never-ending vendetta against the nurses making her bed, penetrated throughout the entire ward; it even penetrated Sister's office, so that its occupant rose from her work at her desk with a sigh, opened the swing doors and made her way down the long ward to where her troublesome patient lay. She was a very pretty girl, tall and slim and nicely curved in her navy uniform. She had corn-coloured hair, cut short and swinging around her neck, with a fringe over her blue eyes and a nose which tilted very slightly above a softly curved mouth so that despite her twenty-six years she reminded anyone meeting her for the first time of a small eager girl wanting to be friendly with everyone.

She reached the bed just as its occupant, sitting in a heap in the middle of it clutching a blanket round her frail person, drew breath to begin on a fresh round of abuse. 'Yer ter leave them blankets,' she shrilled, 'me bed's fine—it don't need making.'

'And what is our Doctor Thorpe going to say when he comes presently and finds you in that untidy heap?' Phyllida Cresswell's voice was quiet and quite unworried by Mrs Gregson's tantrums.

''E won't say nothin', 'e'll be too busy looking at yer pretty face.'

Phyllida wasn't in the least put out. 'There you go again, making up stories. You just wait until I tell his wife!'

Mrs Gregson cackled happily. 'Just me little joke, Sister dear, though you mark my words, some feller'll come along one day and run orf with yer.'

'It sounds exciting,' agreed Phyllida. 'And now how about this bed?'

'Well, if yer say so...'

Phyllida smiled at the old lady, smiled too at the two student nurses and started off down the ward again. It was a good thing that Philip Mount was the Surgical Registrar and rarely came on to her ward; Mrs Gregson's sharp eyes would have spotted that they were rather more than colleagues within minutes. Phyllida frowned slightly. Philip was getting a little too possessive just lately. It wasn't as though they were engaged. Her frown deepened; perhaps it would have been better for them both if they had been, although she couldn't remember that he had ever suggested it, merely taken it for granted that one day they would marry. And he was a good man; there weren't many like him, she knew that; not particularly good-looking, but well built and pleasant-faced and rarely bad-tempered, ready to make allowances for everyone—she wasn't good enough for him and she had told him so on several occasions. But he had only laughed at her, refusing to take her seriously.

She went back into her office and sat down at her desk again and picked up the telephone. There was the laundry to warn about the extra sheets she would need, the dispensary to argue with over the non-arrival of a drug she had ordered, the office to plead with for the loan of a nurse because one of her student nurses had gone off sick—she sighed and lifted the receiver.

The day went badly, with no nurse to replace the one who had gone off sick, two emergencies, Doctor Thorpe's round and him in a nasty temper and not nearly enough clean linen returned from the laundry. Phyllida, a sunny-tempered girl, was decidedly prickly by the time she went to her midday dinner, a state of mind not improved by her friends wanting to know why she was so ratty, and made even worse by one of her friends demanding to know if she had had words with Philip.

'No, I have not,' she declared crossly, and thought suddenly that a good row with him would be better than his even-tempered tolerance when she was feeling ill-humoured. She added rather lamely: 'I've had a foul morning and Doctor Thorpe was in one of his tetchy moods; the round took for ever.'

The talk became general after that and presently, back on the ward, she regained her usual good nature so that Mrs Gregson stopped her as she was going down the ward to say: 'That's better, Sister dear. Black as a thundercloud yer've been all morning.' She grinned, displaying impossibly even false teeth. 'We ain't such a bad lot, are we?'

Phyllida had stopped to lean over the end of her patient's bed. 'You're the nicest lot of ladies I've ever met,' she assured her.

Mrs Gregson nodded, satisfied. 'Going out this evening?' she wanted to know.

Phyllida said that yes, she was and she still had a lot of work to do as she went on her way. She and Philip were going to have dinner with his elder brother and his wife. They lived in Hampstead in a pleasant house; privately she found them a dull couple with two dull children, but they seemed content enough and she had, upon occasion, detected a gleam of envy in Philip's eye at the sight of their comfortable home with its neatly kept garden, well-behaved dog, gleaming furniture and shining windows. She frowned a little as she bent to take her newest patient's blood pressure. It wasn't that she didn't like cleanliness and order and furniture polish, but somehow there was too much of it. She thought with sudden longing of her own home, an old rambling house in a village near Shaftesbury, standing on high ground so that it creaked and groaned in the winter gales and captured all the summer sun there was on its grey stone walls. Her father was the village doctor with a practice scattered miles in every direction and her mother ran the house with the help of old Mrs Drew who was really past it, as well as coping with the large untidy garden, two dogs, a variety of cats, an old pony and some chickens and over and above these such of her four children who might happen to be at home, and they usually brought friends with them.

It was late March, thought Phyllida, neatly charting her findings; the daffodils would be out and the catkins, and in the wilder corners of the garden there would be violets and primroses for the picking. She had a week's holiday due to her, only a few days away now. The thought cheered her enormously and she felt guilty at the relief of getting away from Philip for a little while—perhaps while she was at home she would be able to make up her mind about him. And really, she chided herself as she went from bed to bed, with a nod and a word for the occupants, there should be no need of that. He was a splendid man, generous and honest and thoughtful—he would make a perfect husband. He would be dull too. She wiped the thought from her mind as unworthy and concentrated on his good points so that by the evening when she went off duty she was almost eager to see him.

She took extra pains with her face and hair as she changed out of her uniform and then poked around in her wardrobe. She had clothes enough, for unlike many of her friends she had no need to help out at home, but now she dragged out one dress after the other, dissatisfied with them all, until, pressed for time, she got into a grey wool dress with its matching long coat, tied a bright scarf round her neck, caught up gloves and handbag and skipped down the austere staircase of the Nurses' Home. Philip was waiting in the hospital yard. That was another nice thing about him; he never kept her waiting and he never grumbled if she were late. She smiled widely at him as she got into the elderly Rover he cherished with such care.

'I've had a foul day, Doctor Thorpe was as sour as vinegar and they sent up two chest cases. What about you?' she asked.

'Oh, quite a good list, one or two tacked on, of course, but Sir Hereward was in a good mood.' He turned to smile at her. 'Shall we go to Poon's?'

Phyllida didn't really like Chinese food, but she agreed at once. Poon's was well away from the hospital and not expensive, and although Philip wasn't mean, he hadn't anything other than his salary. They drove through the City, cut into Long Acre and into Cranbourne Street and turned into the Charing Cross Road. There was a good deal of traffic as they turned into Lisle Street and found a parking meter, and the restaurant was crowded too. Phyllida sat down at the corner table found for them and let out a long contented sigh.

'This is nice. I love my work, but it's good to get away from it. I've got a week's holiday in a few days, too.'

'Going home?' Philip was studying the menu.

She chose sweet and sour pork before she replied. 'Yes.' She gave him a questioning look.

'I've a couple of days owing to me...' His nice face beamed at her across the table.

'Then come down for them. I'm going on Sunday evening—when can you manage to get free?'

'Wednesday—until Friday midnight. Your mother won't mind?'

Phyllida laughed. 'You know Mother, she loves a house full—besides, she knows you well enough to hand you a spade and tell you to dig the garden—a nice change from whipping out appendices!'

They spent a pleasant evening together, although thinking about it afterwards, Phyllida had a feeling that they had both been trying too hard; trying in a self-conscious way to turn their rather vague relationship into something more tangible. She couldn't think why, not for herself at any rate. She was fond of Philip but she was almost sure that she didn't want to marry him, and yet her sensible brain told her that he was so right for a husband.

She lay awake for a long time thinking about it and then overslept so that her breakfast was a scrappy affair of tea and toast, and for all the good her sleepless night had done her, she might just as well not have given Philip a thought, and indeed she had no time to think about him at all during the morning. She still had no student nurse to replace the one who had gone off sick and one of the three remaining nurses had gone on holiday. She took the report with outward calm, had a few succinct words with Linda Jenkins, her staff nurse, picked up the pile of post for her patients and started off on her morning round, casting a practised eye over the ward as she went. They might be short-staffed, but the girls were managing very nicely; the beds were being made with all speed and those ladies well enough to get up were being settled into the armchairs arranged at intervals down the long ward, a scheme intended to encourage the convalescent ladies to get together and enjoy a nice chat among themselves. Phyllida had discovered long ago that they became so interested in swapping their illnesses that they forgot to grumble at their own aches and pains, the awful food, the tepid tea, the unfeeling nurses... None of which was true, but she quite understood that they had to have something to gossip about. She paused now by a group and listened to Miss Thompson, a pernicious anaemia who ruled the new patients with a rod of iron since she had been in and out of the ward for years now, describing the operation her sister-in-law had just had. Miss Thompson had the bloodcurdling and quite inaccurate details of it so pat that Phyllida's lovely eyes almost popped out of her head. When Miss Thompson paused for breath she asked drily: 'Did she recover, Miss Thompson?'

She knew that she shouldn't have asked the question; now she would have to listen to a long-drawn-out blow-by-blow account of the unfortunate lady's return to health and strength. She passed around her letters and began a mental assay of the off duty for next week while she stood patiently. When Miss Thompson had at last finished, Phyllida, mindful of hurt feelings, merely remarked that some people had remarkable experiences, admonished the ladies to drink their mid-morning coffee when it arrived and went on her way. She recounted it all to Linda over their own coffee later and chuckled her way into a good humour again, so that when she thought of Philip during a rare few minutes of leisure later that day it was with mild pleasure at the idea of him spending a couple of days at her home.

She only saw him once before she started her leave, and for so short a time that they could only exchange a brief remark as to when he would arrive. She still felt pleased about him coming, but her pleasure was a little dimmed by his matter-of-fact manner, and his 'See you, then' was uttered with the briskness of a brother. True, they had encountered one another in the middle of one of the busiest corridors in the hospital, with nurses, porters and housemen milling up and down, but, thought Phyllida, suddenly annoyed, 'if he loved her as much as he said he did, he could surely have looked at her with rather more feeling?' She left the hospital the following evening, glad that she hadn't seen him again.

She drove down to her home in the neat little Vauxhall Astra, a present from her parents on her twenty-first birthday, five years ago, and although she could have afforded to exchange it she had never felt the need; it went well and she understood it as well as she would ever understand any car. She fastened her seat belt, gave a last glance at the rather grim hospital behind her and drove out into the busy street to meet the London traffic.

It took her quite some time to get out of London and on to the M3, but she was a good driver and not impatient. Once on the motorway she sent the small car racing along and at its end, took the A30 to Salisbury. It was almost empty of traffic by now

and she made good time to the town, working round
it to the north and picking up the A30 again on its
further side. She was on home ground now and although it was getting on for ten o'clock, she didn't
feel tired. Just short of Shaftesbury she turned off
on to the Tisbury road and then turned again, going
through pleasantly wooded country and climbing a
little on the winding road. Over the brow of the hill
she slowed for a minute. The lights of Gifford Ferris
twinkled at her almost at its foot, not many lights,
for the village was small and off the main road. But
it was by no means isolated; there were other villages within a mile or two on all sides; any number
of outlying farms and main roads to the north and
south. Phyllida put her foot down and sent the car
scuttling down the hill and then more slowly into
the village's main street. It had a small market
square with a stone cross in its centre, a handful of
shops around it besides a comfortable hotel, and at
the top of the hill on the other side one or two old
stone houses. She stopped before one of these and
jumped out, but before she could reach the door it
had been flung open.

'Your mother's in the kitchen, getting your supper,' observed her father placidly. 'Nice to see you,
my dear—did you have a good trip?'

She kissed him soundly. 'Super—almost no traffic

once I'd left London. Something smells good—I'm famished! I'll get my case...'

'Run along and find your mother, I'll bring it in. The car will be all right there until the morning.'

Phyllida walked down the long narrow hall and opened the kitchen door at its end, contentedly sniffing the air; furniture polish, the scent from a bowl of hyacinths on a table, and fragrant cooking. They spelled home.

Her mother was at the scrubbed table in the middle of the room, cutting bread. She looked up as Phyllida went in, dropped the knife and came to meet her. 'Darling—how lovely to see you, and how nice you look in that suit. There's watercress soup and mushroom omelette and buttered toast and tea, though Father says you're to have a glass of sherry first. He'll bring it presently.' She returned Phyllida's hug and added: 'Willy's here just for a few days—half term, you know.'

The younger of her two brothers appeared as her mother spoke, a boy of fourteen, absurdly like his father, with tousled hair and an air of never having enough to eat. He bore this out with a brotherly: 'Hi, Sis, heard you come, guessed there'd be food.'

She obligingly sat down at the table and shared her supper while their mother cut bread and wondered aloud how many more meals he would want before he settled to sleep.

'I'm growing,' he pointed out cheerfully, 'and look at Phylly—she finished growing years ago and she's stuffing herself.'

'Rude boy,' observed his sister placidly. 'How's school?'

Her father came in then and they sat around, all talking at once until Willy was sent off to bed and Phyllida and her mother tidied the kitchen, washed up and went to the sitting room with a tray of coffee.

It was a pleasant room; long and low-ceilinged and furnished with some nice pieces which had been in the family for generations. There was comfort too; easy chairs drawn up to the open fire, a vast sofa with a padded back and plenty of small reading lamps. Phyllida curled up on the sofa, the firelight warm on her face and dutifully answered the questions with which her mother bombarded her. They were mostly about Philip and cunningly put, and she answered them patiently, wishing illogically that her mother didn't seem so keen on him all of a sudden. She had been vaguely put out after Philip's first visit to her home by her mother's reaction to him. 'Such a nice young man,' her parent had declared, 'and so serious. I'm sure if you marry him he'll make a model husband.' It hadn't been the words so much as the tone in which they had been uttered, and ever since Phyllida had been worried by a faint niggling doubt at the back of her pretty head; a model husband sounded so dull. But this evening she could detect no doubt in her mother's voice—indeed, her parent chattered on at some length about Phyllida's future, talking about the wedding as though it were already a certainty.

Phyllida finished her coffee, observed rather tartly that no one had asked her to get married yet and when her mother remarked that she had understood that Philip was coming to stay for a couple of days, pointed out very quickly that it was only a friendly visit—it made a nice restful change after his work at the hospital. Mrs Cresswell agreed placidly, her still pretty head bent over some embroidery, and presently Phyllida went to bed.

Being home was delightful—pottering in the garden, helping her mother round the house, going for long bike rides with Willy, helping in her father's surgery. Phyllida relaxed, colour came back into her London-pale cheeks, her hair seemed more golden, her eyes bluer. Her mother, looking at her as she made pastry at the kitchen table, felt certain that Philip would ask her to marry him when he came.

She was right; he did, but not at once. He wasn't a man to rush his fences, and it wasn't until the morning of his second day there that he suggested that they might go into Shaftesbury for her mother and do some shopping, and Phyllida, called in from fetching the eggs from the hen-house at the end of the garden, readily agreed. She had been glad to see Philip when he had arrived, but not, she confessed to herself, thrilled, but they had quickly slipped into their pleasant, easygoing camaraderie and he was an undemanding companion. She put a jacket on over her slacks, combed her fringe, added a little more lipstick and pronounced herself ready.

Shaftesbury was full of people and cars; it always was, probably because it was a small town and built originally on top of a hill and its shops were concentrated in two main streets. They had done their shopping, chosen a variety of cakes from the fragrant bakery hidden away in an alley where the two streets met, and sat themselves down in the buttery of one of the few hotels for a cup of coffee before Philip made any but the most impersonal remarks.

'Wouldn't you like to leave hospital and have a home of your own?' he wanted to know.

Phyllida chose a bun, not paying as much attention as she should have done. 'Oh, yes,' she said casually, 'I'd love it. Have a bun?'

'Then why don't you?'

She looked up then, suddenly realizing what he was going to say. 'Don't, Philip—please...'

He took a bun too. 'Why not? You must know that I want to marry you?'

'Yes—well, yes, I suppose I did, but not—not urgently.'

He was a very honest young man. 'If you mean I'm beside myself with impatience to get married, you're right. But I've given the matter a great deal of thought lately and I'm sure you're the wife for me; we know each other very well by now and I'm more than half in love with you.' He smiled at her across the table. 'How about it, Phylly?'

She knew that she was going to say no. Perhaps, she thought desperately, she had never intended to say anything else, but it was going to be hard to say it. For one thing, she was strongly tempted to accept Philip's matter-of-fact proposal. They would live together happily enough, she would take an interest in his work and he would be a kind and considerate husband, of that she was sure. She would have a pleasant enough life with enough to live on, a nice home, friends of her own sort and children. She would like several children; only she had the lowering feeling that Philip would want a neat little family of a boy and a girl. He would be a splendid father too and the children would be good, obedient and reasonably clever. In fact, life wouldn't be what she had dreamed—a vague dream of a man who would sweep her off her feet, treasure her and love her and never on any account allow her to wear the trousers, and more than that, would fill his house with a brood of healthy, naughty children.

She sighed and said gently: 'It wouldn't work, Philip.'

He showed no rancour. 'Why not? You must have reasons.'

She frowned. 'I like you very, very much—I think for a while I was a little in love with you, but I'm sure that it's not enough.' She looked at him with unhappy blue eyes. 'I'm sorry, Philip—and I don't think I shall change my mind.'

He said calmly: 'You're in love with someone else?'

'No. Oh, no, no one at all, that's why it's difficult...you see, you're so right for me. I respect you and admire your work and the way you live, and I like being with you, only I don't want to marry you.' She added miserably: 'It would be such a mistake, and the awful thing is I don't know what I want.'

Philip finished his coffee with the air of a man who wasn't in the least defeated. 'I'm not taking no for an answer,' he told her quietly. 'I won't bother you, but I'll wait.'

'But it won't be any good.' She looked like an unhappy little girl, her short upper lip caught between her teeth, her eyes enormous under the fringe. She felt suddenly peevish. If she could get away, right away, he would forget her because he didn't love her, not with the sort of love which just didn't want to go on living without her—he might even fall in love with someone else quite quickly. It struck her then that he was the kind of man who didn't need to love like that; he was a calm, even-tempered man and too much love would choke him. When he only smiled and offered her more coffee she didn't say any more, for what was the use?

Philip didn't allow her refusal to make any difference between them. He spent the rest of the day with her, treating her with the same good-natured affection that he had always shown her. He went back to London that day after tea, saying all the right things to her mother and father and reminding Phyllida cheerfully that they would be going to the Annual Dance at the hospital together two days after her return: 'Though I'll see you before then,' he had assured her.

She watched him go with mixed feelings; real regret that she didn't love him and a faint touch of temper because he seemed so unmoved about her refusal—or was he so sure that she would give in? The thought made her even more peevish.

The moment he was out of sight her mother remarked: 'Well, dear, are you going to marry him? I'm sure he must have asked you.'

Phyllida hadn't meant to say anything about it—not just yet anyway, but she perceived now that her mother would go on gently asking questions until she got an answer.

'Yes, he did, and I said no.'

'Oh, good.' Mrs Cresswell took no notice of her daughter's surprised look. 'He's a very nice man, darling, but not your sort.'

'What is my sort, Mother?' Phyllida didn't feel peevish any more.

Her mother washed a tea-cup with care; it was old and treasured like most of the china she insisted on using every day. 'Well, he doesn't have to be handsome, but eye-catching, if you know what I mean, the sort of man who would take command in a sticky situation and know just what to do—and not let you have your own way unless he thought it was good for you.'

'A bigheaded tyrant,' suggested Phyllida.

'No, dear, just a man who would never take you for granted; take great care of you without you ever knowing it, and know exactly what he intended doing with his life—and yours, of course.'

'A paragon. Mother, I never knew you were romantic—does Father know?'

'He married me,' observed her parent placidly. 'What will you do about Philip? I mean, you can't help but see him often, can you?'

Phyllida had piled the tea things on to a tray, on her way to putting them away in the carved corner cupboard in the sitting room. 'I hadn't thought of that,' she said slowly. 'It would be sense to leave, I suppose.'

'Well, think about it, darling.' Her mother spoke briskly. 'It could be done easily enough.'

Phyllida gave her a faintly mocking look. 'Mother, you have no idea...'

'No, dear, but things can always be done, however awkward, if only one applies oneself to them.'

Nothing more was said after that. Phyllida went back to London two days later, reluctant to give up a job she liked and go through all the fuss and bother of finding another one—and outside London, she supposed gloomily.

She didn't see Philip until the evening of the dance; indeed, she had taken care to keep out of his way, going to great lengths to avoid their usual meeting places, keeping one eye on the ward door in case he should come to see a patient referred for surgery.

But she had to see him again eventually. They met in the entrance hall, shortly after the dance had started, he very correct in his black tie, she prettier than ever in a pearly grey chiffon dress and silver slippers.

Her hullo was a trifle awkward, but Philip didn't seem to notice. He took her arm, asked her where she'd been during the last two days and suggested that they went into the big lecture hall, decorated for the occasion, and danced. It wasn't until they had circled the place at least twice that he asked: 'Had second thoughts, Phylly?'

'About what?' And then, despising herself for the remark: 'No, I haven't, Philip, and I'm not going to—truly I'm not.'

He laughed down at her. 'No? Shall we wait and see? We meet most days, don't we, so it won't be a case of "Out of sight, out of mind"—you're very used to me being there, aren't you?'

She met his eyes. 'Yes. You mean you'll wear me away like water on a stone.'

'Nicely put, although I wouldn't describe you as stony. You'll change your mind.'

Perhaps it was because he looked so smug and sure of himself that she resolved then and there to look for another job. She didn't say anything though, but danced the night away, mostly with Philip but with all the other men she knew as well. She enjoyed herself too; tomorrow was time enough to think things out.

She hadn't got much further by the following evening when she came off duty. It had been a busy day with several of her patients not doing as well as she had hoped, so that she felt too depressed to do more than take off her cap and put her feet up on the sofa in the Sisters' sitting room. She closed her eyes the better to think and then opened them again as the door opened and Meg Dawson, Surgical Ward Sister and one of her closest friends, came in. 'There's a phone call for you, Phylly—your mum.'

Phyllida had taken her shoes off as well. She padded down the passage to the phone box at its end and picked up the receiver. Her mother's voice, very youthful still, sounded very clear. 'Phylly? Father wants to talk to you.'

Phyllida was surprised; she and her father got on splendidly, but he was a busy man, not given to telephone conversations unless they concerned a patient. She said cautiously: 'Yes?'

Doctor Cresswell didn't waste time. 'You mentioned leaving, Phylly—if you do, there's a job going in about three weeks' time.'

A sign from heaven, thought Phyllida childishly. 'I could leave then—I've still another week's leave due, so I'd have to work three weeks notice...' She knew that her father was nodding his head even though he didn't speak. 'What sort of job?'

'A patient of mine until I referred her to Sir Keith Maltby—I attend her parents too. A girl of eighteen with erythroblastic leukaemia—I wasn't called in until she had been ill for some time, sent her straight to Sir Keith who got her into hospital; she was there two months, had several courses of cytotoxic drugs and has improved considerably, gained weight, taken an interest in life. Her mother came to see me

today, says Gaby has set her heart on going to somewhere sunny—they want to take her on a short
cruise—Madeira and the Canaries, but they want a
skilled nurse to keep an eye on her and recognise
the signs and symptoms if she should have a relapse.
All expenses paid, and fare of course, and a decent
salary—about three weeks, they think. Of course
you realise that Gaby hasn't very long to live. Sir
Keith agrees with me that she should be allowed to
do what she wants within reason—her parents are
wealthy, fortunately. It would get you away, my
dear, if that's what you want.' And when Phyllida
didn't answer: 'I could arrange for you to see these
people—the name's de Wolff—they've booked for
a cruise leaving on April the sixth, that's not quite
four weeks away.'

Phyllida heard herself say that yes, she would like
to meet the de Wolffs and that provided they liked
her, she would be prepared to take the job. 'I've a
couple of days off, but not till the end of the week,
that would be too late to give in my notice—look,
Father, I'm off at five o'clock tomorrow and on at
one o'clock the next day. I'll drive down in the evening, see them in the morning and drive straight
back—I can just do it provided they'll make an appointment early in the morning.'

'Splendid, my dear. I'll see to it and ring you
back.'

So she found herself the next day rushing off duty, racing into her outdoor things and driving as fast as traffic permitted out of London. The appointment was for half past nine on the following morning and to save time she was to go to the de Wolffs' house, as it was on the London side of Shaftesbury and she could drive straight on back to work after the interview. She hadn't told anyone about it and she hadn't seen Philip. She had toyed with the idea of going to the office and giving in her notice that morning, but there was always the chance that the job wouldn't turn out to be what she expected. She got clear of London at last and belted for home.

CHAPTER TWO

MRS CRESSWELL was waiting with supper, and her father came from his study to talk to Phyllida while she ate it. 'Gaby's a nice enough girl, poor child—difficult at times, I gather from her mother, but it has to be remembered that she's very ill. She has no idea how ill, of course, although her parents have been told. Not that they've accepted it well; they simply cannot believe that a girl of eighteen can die. They're both energetic, social types and can't understand why Gaby isn't the same.'

Phyllida carved another slice of her mother's home-baked bread. 'You don't like them,' she stated flatly.

'I wouldn't go as far as to say that, shall I say that I regret their attitude towards illness and death—two inconvenient states they simply refuse to recognise, but I'm glad they're so eager to take Gaby on this trip. Sir Keith tells me it's only a question of three months or so.'

'Oh, Father, how awful—isn't there anything at all to be done?'

He shook his head. 'You know that yourself, my dear. Thank heaven it's extremely rare—other forms of leukaemia have a much more favourable prognosis these days.'

Phyllida left home after breakfast the next morning, to drive the few miles to the de Wolffs' home. She joined the main Salisbury road presently and then turned away on to a country road leading to Berwick St John, and after another mile came upon the house she was looking for. It was Edwardian, much gabled and ornamented with beams and plasterwork in an attempt to make it look Tudor. It was large too, spick and span as to paintwork and altogether too perfect for her taste. She thought with sudden nostalgia of her own home only a few miles away and so very different, its ancient oak door almost always open, its mullioned windows wide, with curtains blowing a welcome. There were no curtains to be seen here and no open windows.

She got out, crossed the gravel, so smooth that she felt guilty treading on it, and rang the bell. The man-servant who opened the door matched the house exactly; correct; unwelcoming and without any warmth. He begged her to enter, ushered her into a small panelled room furnished with expensive, tasteless furniture, and went away.

Both Mr and Mrs de Wolff entered the room a moment later, bringing with them an air of brisk efficiency and charm. They bade Phyllida seat herself, and without any preliminaries, proceeded to put her—as Mr de Wolff observed—in the picture. 'You shall see Gaby presently,' promised Mrs de Wolff, and smiled charmingly at Phyllida. She was a handsome woman, in her forties but not looking it by reason of exquisite make-up and beautifully cut hair, and a casual tweed suit which must have cost a great deal of money. She smiled a lot, thought Phyllida, and she quite understood what her father had meant when he had told her that neither she nor her husband wanted to accept the fact that Gaby's illness was a terminal one.

'The specialist takes a grave view, of course,' said Mr de Wolff, teetering on his toes before the fireplace, like the chairman of a board meeting, 'but we're both so healthy ourselves we take a more optimistic view. This little holiday should do her the world of good, and she's so keen to go.'

'You will notify the ship's doctor of her illness?' asked Phyllida, 'and I should want her medical notes with me so that they can be referred to if necessary.'

Mrs de Wolff frowned, and just for a minute all the charm had gone, but it was back almost at once. 'Of course we'll see to all that, Miss Cresswell, you can safely leave us to arrange everything just as it should be. We shall consult Sir Keith, of course—such a pity that he's in Scotland, otherwise you could have gone to see him, but I'm sure your father has told you all there is to know about Gaby.' She got to her feet. 'Would you like to see her now before you go? We do so hope you'll come with us, but it's for you to decide of course.'

She crossed the room and rang the bell and when the unsmiling manservant came, asked him to let Miss Gaby know that she was wanted in the morning room.

The first thing Phyllida thought when she saw Gaby was how very pretty she was, small and slim to the point of thinness and far too pale, with a cloud of dark hair to match her dark eyes. This thought was followed at once by a second one, that the girl looked far more ill than her parents had made out. She seemed a docile little creature too, replying meekly to her mother's remarks about how much she wanted to go on holiday with them, and what she intended to do. But she offered no remarks of her own, although she smiled at Phyllida and went on smiling when her father said that she was a spoilt girl and had everything she could possibly want. He sounded very pleased with himself as he said it, and Phyllida wondered if he had stopped to think that having everything one wanted wasn't much use if one wasn't going to be alive to enjoy it.

She stayed for another half an hour, asking questions as discreetly as possible as to her duties. It would be mostly companionship, she gathered, and the giving of Gaby's medicines and pills, as well as

a number of small routine tasks—temperature and
pulse and blood pressure and making sure that her
patient slept well. She rose to go presently, reiter-
ating that she would want the case notes with her,
and reminding the de Wolffs that the ship's doctor
would have to be informed. Gaby had gone with
some small excuse so that Phyllida could speak
openly now. A little uneasy because of the de
Wolffs' casual attitude towards their daughter's illness, she said gently: 'You do know that Gaby is
very ill? I know it's hard to believe—and you're
quite happy about her making this trip?'

Mrs de Wolff's charming smile slipped again.
'Quite happy, Miss Cresswell,' she said with final-
ity. So Phyllida left it at that, only staying to arrange
to meet them all on the morning of the sixth.

'We shall be driving up,' explained Mr de Wolff.
'We'll pick you up at the hospital, that will be the
easiest way, I think.'

They wished her goodbye, and the manservant
ushered her out into the chilly March morning. She
had driven for ten minutes or so when she said out
loud: 'Well, they could at least have offered me a
cup of coffee!'

She reached Salisbury by continuing along the
same country road from the de Wolffs' house, stopping on the way to have the cup of coffee no one

had offered her, and once through Salisbury she made for London without waste of time.

At the hospital she had the leisure to change into uniform, write out her resignation and present herself at the office. The Senior Nursing Officer was considerably astonished, but in the course of her long and successful career she had learned when not to ask questions. Beyond expressing a sincere regret at Phyllida's decision to leave, she said nothing other than to wish her a successful future and advise her to give the office due warning as to the exact date of her departure.

'You have a week's holiday still, Sister Cresswell, and I expect you can arrange to add your days off to that. I shall have to appoint someone in your place, but in the meantime I think that Staff Nurse Jenkins is quite capable of carrying on. Do you agree?'

'She's very good, Miss Cutts, and the patients like her. The nurses work well for her too.'

'In that case I see no reason why she shouldn't apply for the post.' Miss Cutts nodded kindly in gracious dismissal.

Phyllida, speeding to the ward, felt intense surprise at what she had done. Probably if she had stopped to think about it, she would have decided against leaving, but now it was done she felt relief as well. She still had to see Philip and explain, but she would bide her time and choose the right moment for that.

But the matter was taken out of her hands. He came on to the ward to take a look at a suspected duodenal ulcer which would probably need operation, and instead of leaving at once he followed Phyllida to her office, shut the door behind him and asked her quietly: 'What's this I hear about you leaving?'

'Oh, dear—so soon?' She turned to face him across the small room. 'I only saw Miss Cutts half an hour ago and I haven't told a soul—I was going to talk to you about it, Philip.' She pushed her cap away from her forehead. 'Not now, though—I've heaps to do.'

'You're off at five o'clock? I'll meet you at Tony's at half past six.' He went away without another word, leaving her to wonder for the rest of the day if she had made the mistake of her lifetime. Even now, if he overwhelmed her...she wondered at the back of her mind if he felt strongly enough about her to do that. With a tremendous effort she dismissed the whole thing and attacked her work; there was enough of that to keep her mind off other things; the duodenal ulcer not responding to medical treatment; Mrs Gregson springing a mild coronary upon them; the young girl in the corner bed with undulant fever, so depressed that no one knew what to do next to get her cheerful again, and the sixteen-year-old anorexia nervosa next to her, taking precious time and patience with every unwanted meal...

Tony's was a small unassuming restaurant within five minutes' walk of the hospital and much patronised by the doctors and nurses. Phyllida arrived punctually and found a table for two by one of the windows. There was no view, only the drab street outside, and she sat staring at it until Philip slid into the seat opposite her.

His 'Hullo—shall we have the usual?' was uttered in his normal calm way and when she nodded: 'And now what's all this nonsense about leaving?'

'It's not nonsense, Philip. I've given Miss Cutts my notice and I leave in three weeks' time—just under, as a matter of fact. And I've got a job.'

Just for a moment his calm was shaken. 'A job? So you'd arranged it all some time ago?'

'No.' She explained carefully and added: 'I'm sorry, Philip, I like you very much, I told you that, but the best thing to do is for us to stop seeing each other.'

He said with faint smugness, 'You're afraid I'll wear you down.'

She stared at him, her blue eyes clear and honest. 'I don't know,' she told him earnestly, 'but if you did, it wouldn't be right.'

The waitress brought them the soup of the day and Phyllida studied it as though it was something of vital importance. Presently she said: 'It's difficult to explain, but when I marry I want to be so in love with the man that nothing else matters; there'd be no doubts and no wondering about the future and where we'd live or how.' She looked up from her soup and gazed at him from under her fringe.

'And you don't feel like that about me? Phylly, grow up! You're living in a fairy tale—there's no such thing as that kind of love, only in romantic novels. I'm surprised at you, I thought you were such a sensible, matter-of-fact girl, with no nonsense about you.'

Phyllida picked up her spoon and gave the Heinz tomato a stir. That was the trouble, she thought silently, he'd got her all wrong. She was romantic and full of nonsense; he had confused the practical, sensible young woman who ran the medical ward so efficiently with her real self, and looking at him now, she could see that he still thought it.

He was half way through his soup by now. 'Well, trot off if you must,' he told her cheerfully, 'and come back when you're ready. I daresay I'll still be here.'

She sat silently while the soup was replaced by pork chops, frozen peas and a pile of chips which might have daunted any girl but her, who ate like a horse and never put on an inch. When the waitress had gone again, she said patiently: 'I'm not coming back; this job is only for three weeks—I don't know what I'll do after that.'

It annoyed her that he still looked complacent, but to say more wasn't going to help. Deeds, not words, she told herself silently.

'What is this job?' he wanted to know.

She told him, and being an opportunist, picked his brains. 'I don't know a great deal about it—I've never seen a case, though I've nursed one or two lymphoblastic leukaemias and they did rather well.'

'This one isn't likely to—it's rare, so rare that there aren't enough statistics, but it's a terminal illness, I'm afraid. Have you got the notes yet?'

'No. Sir Keith Maltby has been looking after her, but he's in Scotland. Father will get the notes from him, though, he's already telephoned him about it. He doesn't object to Gaby going on this cruise—he says she can do what she likes provided her parents understand that the moment she shows signs of deterioration they must get her to hospital or fly her back without delay. The ship's doctor will have all the facts; Mr de Wolff has undertaken to see about that. There's plenty of money, I believe, so there's no reason why anything should go wrong from that side of it.'

As she spoke, she wondered uneasily why she

didn't quite believe what she was saying. Perhaps because she had taken a faint dislike to Mr and Mrs de Wolff—quite an unfounded one, based entirely on his brisk attitude towards his daughter's illness, and his wife's calculated charm. Phyllida gave herself a mental shake, agreed with Philip that it would be interesting to see Madeira and the Canaries even if her chance to do so might be limited, and then applied herself to responding suitably to his unshakable friendliness.

It remained unshakable too for the next few weeks, and she felt guilty because she was unable to feel regret at her decision, largely because Philip made no secret of the fact that he expected her to come running once she had brought Gaby back home again.

'Any ideas about the next job?' he asked her airily. 'A bit difficult while you're away, isn't it? It'll mean an enforced holiday while you find something to suit you and then go after it. You might not get it either.' He sounded so satisfied that she could cheerfully have thrown something at him.

Leaving the ward was harder than leaving Philip, she discovered; she had grown fond of it during the last few years; it was old and awkward to work in and there were never enough staff, but she had loved the ever-changing succession of patients, and some of those, like old Mrs Gregson, were so upset at her

going that she had promised that she would come
and visit them the moment she got back from the
cruise. Unthinkingly she had mentioned that to
Philip and been furious with herself for doing so
when she saw the knowing little smile on his face,
smugly sure that she was making an excuse to return
to the hospital and see him. She managed not to see
too much of him, though, going home for her days
off so that she might collect Gaby's notes and listen
to her father's sound advice, as well as root around
in her bedroom to see what clothes she should take
with her. It would be warm for most of the time and
last year's summer dresses looked depressingly dull.
She decided to travel in a jersey suit and the silk
blouse she had bought in a fit of extravagance, pack
some slacks and tops and buy one or two things in
London.

There was a nice selection of cruise clothes; her
modest list lengthened as she went along the rails.
In the end she left the shop with a new bikini, three
cotton dresses, sleeveless and light as air, and because they were so pretty, two evening dresses, one
in pink crêpe with not much top and a wide floating
skirt, and the other of white organza. She wasn't
sure if she would have the chance to wear them, but
there was no harm in taking them along. She already
had a flowery-patterned long skirt and several pretty

tops to go with it and a couple of short silky dresses from last year.

She packed her bags, arranged to have the rest of her luggage sent home, bade goodbye to her friends at a rather noisy party after the day's work, and retired to bed, but not to sleep at once. There was too much to think about—Gaby and her treatment and the still vague disquiet because she didn't know too much about it, although the notes were comprehensive enough and her father had primed her well. Presumably the ship's doctor would keep a close eye on her patient, and after all, her parents would be there. Slightly reassured, Phyllida allowed her thoughts to turn to Philip. She had contrived to bid him good-bye at the party, with people milling around them so that there was very little chance to say much. She had tried to sound final, but he hadn't believed her. It was annoying and she worried about it, getting sleepier and sleepier until she nodded off at last.

She left the hospital in some state, for the de Wolffs arrived for her in a chauffeur-driven Cadillac; it took up a lot of room in the forecourt and Phyllida, turning to wave to such of her friends who had managed to spare the time to look out of their ward windows, saw their appreciative grins. She got in beside the chauffeur after a final wave and caught Mrs de Wolff's eye. It didn't look in the least friendly and she wondered why, but she smiled at Mr de Wolff, and spoke to Gaby, who answered her eagerly and with encouraging warmth. Phyllida, a charitable girl who seldom thought ill of anyone, supposed Mrs de Woolff had had a trying time getting ready for their holiday. She settled herself in her seat, resolving to do her best to see that Gaby wasn't only well looked after, but kept amused too, so that her parents could enjoy themselves too.

They arrived at the dock with only a very short time to spare before embarking—done deliberately, Mr de Wolff explained, so that there would be no delays for Gaby in getting on board. Phyllida took her patient's arm as they walked slowly up the gangway, for Gaby looked exhausted, then followed the steward up to the Sun Deck. They were to share a de luxe cabin and she looked around her with deep satisfaction; she was used to the normal comforts of life, but this was luxury. She sat Gaby down in a comfortable chair, noted with satisfaction that their luggage was already waiting for them, and took a quick look round.

The cabin was large, even for the two of them, with beds widely spaced, a comfortable sofa, a table and two easy chairs. The window was large and the lighting well arranged and the adjoining bathroom all she could have wished for. It only needed a pleasant stewardess to offer to unpack for them to complete her satisfaction, but she declined this service and asked instead if they could have a tray of tea, for Gaby looked as though she could do with something of the sort. It was barely midday and Mr de Wolff had told her they would be going to the second sitting for their meals, still an hour and a half away; ample time to unpack, check unobtrusively that Gaby was fit to go to the restaurant, and try to get to know her better.

They drank their tea without interruption. The de Wolffs hadn't appeared; probably they realised that Gaby was tired and needed to rest. Phyllida unpacked for both of them, not bothering her patient to talk. After lunch she would search out the doctor, show him the notes and ask for any instructions he might care to give her. Gaby could rest on her bed in the mean-time. The girl looked fagged out and Phyllida frowned a little; the job was full of uncertainties and Gaby was a very sick girl. She wondered again if it had been wise of her parents to allow her to come on the cruise and then conceded that if the girl had set her heart on it and had so little time to live, they were only doing what any loving parents would want to do. It was a pity that Sir Keith hadn't seen Gaby for some weeks, but the de Wolffs had said that he had agreed to the trip, so it must be reasonably safe for Gaby to go. Phyllida dismissed her gloomy thoughts and started to chat quietly, hanging away her patient's lovely clothes as she did so.

They shared a table with Mr and Mrs de Wolff at lunch, both of whom dominated the conversation, talking animatedly about the places they were to visit, the various entertainments on board and how splendid it all was for Gaby, who ate almost no lunch, replied docilely when she was spoken to, and attracted a good many admiring glances from the surrounding tables.

Phyllida did too, although she wasn't aware of it; she was too concerned about her patient.

The meal was a leisurely one, passengers serving themselves from a long buffet of cold meats and salads, arranged in mouthwatering abundance. Gaby's parents didn't seem to notice that she was drooping with fatigue, so that Phyllida took affairs into her own hands and when the steward brought the coffee, excused both herself and Gaby, whisked her to their cabin, tucked her up on her bed, and went in search of the doctor's surgery.

It was three decks down, adjacent to a small hospital. The doctor was at his desk, a young man with a pleasant open face, talking to the ship's nurse. Phyllida took a dislike to her on sight and felt that the feeling was reciprocated; she didn't like heavy make-up and brightly tinted nails on a nurse, nor did she fancy the hard blue eyes and tight mouth in what should have been a pretty face. However, her errand wasn't with the nurse. She introduced herself briskly, stated her business and waited for the doctor to speak.

He looked bewildered. 'But I haven't heard...' he began. 'I've had no information about this Miss de Wolff. Perhaps you'll tell me about her, Miss—er—Cresswell.'

It took a little time, although she gave the information concisely and without personal comment. When she had finished he said thoughtfully: 'Of course I'll look after her and do everything in my power to help. You say she's entered a period remission? Then it's quite possible that she'll be able to enjoy this cruise, to a limited extent, of course—and return home at least none the worse. May I keep these notes and study them? I'll see that you get them back. Perhaps if I were to call and see Miss de Wolff...this evening, or later this afternoon after tea?'

Phyllida agreed. 'I thought we'd have tea in the cabin and then dress without hurrying.'

'Very wise. I think you should suit your activities to her mood. You say she insisted on coming on this holiday?'

'Well, yes, so her parents told me—perhaps it was just a flash in the pan; she's not shown anything but a—a kind of docile acceptance.'

The doctor rose to his feet. 'Would you like me to talk to her parents?'

Phyllida considered. 'If when you've seen her you think it necessary, yes, please.' She hesitated. 'They seem to think that this cruise will put her on her feet again. They can't accept...'

'I know—it's hard for people to realise. Miss de Wolff has no inkling?'

'None that I know of, but I don't know her very well yet. I'll tell you if I think she has.'

They parted in friendly fashion and Phyllida started off down the long corridor taking her to the other end of the ship, to be overtaken almost at once by the nurse.

'I thought I'd let you know that you'd better not expect too much help from me,' she began. 'I have quite a busy time, you know, and I have to be on call round the clock.'

Phyllida stopped to look at her. 'That's OK, I'm sure you must be pretty busy. I don't expect I'll need any help, thanks all the same.'

The other girl gave the suggestion of a sniff. 'If you need any advice...' she began.

Phyllida's large blue eyes flashed. 'I expect I'll be able to cope,' she said gently. 'I've been Medical Ward Sister at St Michael's for four years.' She smiled widely, added 'goodbye' and went on her way, her blonde hair flying round cheeks which were a little pinker than usual, by reason of her vexation.

The doctor was very good with Gaby, matter-of-fact and friendly, taking care not to alarm her by questions which might give her reason to think. And afterwards, on the pretext of fetching some pills in case Gaby felt seasick, Phyllida went back to the surgery.

He said heavily: 'Well, Miss Cresswell, if she'd been my daughter I'd never for one moment entertained the idea of her coming on a trip like this, however much she'd set her heart on it. And she's not wildly enthusiastic about it, is she? Is she spoilt? She didn't strike me as being so.'

Phyllida shook her head. 'I don't think so. She's very quiet and agrees with everything her parents suggest.' She didn't add the unspoken thought that Gaby appeared to be in considerable awe of her parents and anxious, almost painfully so, to please them.

'Well, I'll have a word with them and take a look at her each day. You'll come to me at once if you think it necessary, won't you?'

Phyllida felt better after that, and after due thought went along to the de Wolffs' cabin. It surprised her to discover that they were put out over her visit to the doctor. 'There was really no need,' declared Mrs de Wolff sharply. 'Gaby is a little tired, but otherwise she's recovering very well. We don't want ideas put into her head.'

'I don't think anyone will do that, Mrs de Wolff—after all, she's been under a doctor for so long now, she can't find it strange if the ship's doctor pays her a visit.' She turned to Mr de Wolff. 'I thought you were going to tell him about Gaby—he knew nothing at all about her.'

'I considered it unnecessary.' Mr de Wolff spoke pompously and looked annoyed. 'After all, if Sir Keith gave his consent to this cruise, I hardly suppose that we lesser mortals need to interfere.'

Phyllida went pink. 'I have no intention of interfering, Mr de Wolff, but Gaby has a severe illness and you asked me to look after her and I intend to do so. How long ago is it since Sir Keith Maltby actually saw her?'

Her employer went a rich plum colour. 'That's beside the point, Miss Cresswell. All we ask is that you carry out your duties.'

Phyllida drew a calming breath. She was wasting time; he had no intention of telling her. 'Where would you like us to meet you before dinner?'

She heard his sigh of relief. 'Oh, in the Neptune Bar—about eight o'clock.'

Gaby seemed better when Phyllida got back to their cabin, and became quite animated over the choice of the dress she should wear. She decided on a plain, long-sleeved blue silk sheath, for no one would dress on the first night at sea, and Phyllida put on one of last year's dresses, a very plain one; she considered it made her look just as a nurse out of uniform should look.

The evening went off very well after all. The doctor had introduced himself to the de Wolffs in the bar, offered his services should they be required and went away before the two girls arrived, and if Gaby didn't eat a good dinner, at least she seemed to be enjoying herself. All the same, she went quite willingly to bed when Phyllida suggested it, and Phyllida, quite tired out, went too.

The days formed a pleasant pattern; they breakfasted in their cabin and then spent a leisurely morning sitting on deck, and if Phyllida regretted not being able to join in the deck games and wander off to chat to some of the other passengers, she didn't admit it, even to herself. It worried her that they saw so little of Gaby's parents, who seemed to think that meeting their daughter at lunch and dinner was sufficient, nor did they express anxiety over her condition or ask Phyllida how she was progressing. Luckily the weather was calm and getting warmer, so that by Sunday morning they were able to wear cotton dresses and lie in the sun for a time. It was while they were doing this that the doctor joined them for their mid-morning beef tea and Phyllida, in a casual voice masking her worry, mentioned Gaby's headache. 'Quite a troublesome one,' she added lightly, 'it just doesn't go away.'

'Ah, yes—one of those sick headaches, I expect,' observed the doctor, taking his cue smartly.

Gaby nodded listlessly. 'Yes, I was sick in the night—Phylly had to get up—that's why I feel so dozy now.'

The doctor didn't stay long, and presently, while Gaby slept, Phyllida went in search of him. 'Do you think it's infiltration of the meninges?' she asked anxiously. 'My father told me about that. Should I tell her parents? She seemed so much better—we haven't done much, but she was beginning to eat a little and take an interest in things.'

'Where are her parents?'

'They play bridge a good deal of the time and they've made a good many friends.'

'They don't see much of Gaby? Not enough to notice if she's better or worse?'

'No.'

'I'll have a word with them if you like, and I'll have another look at her later on. I don't like the headache and sickness, it may possibly be what you suggest.'

By the evening Gaby was worse, the headache was persistent now and so was the sickness, and she had become irritable, so that nothing Phyllida could

say or do was right. And when the doctor came to
see her just before dinner he looked grave. 'I'm going to advise you to disembark at Madeira,' he said.
'There's a good hospital there, and while I don't
think she needs to go there at the moment, if you
were to stay in an hotel she could be moved quickly.
Better still, her parents could fly her back home
straight away. I don't think she should stay on
board, we haven't the facilities.'

Phyllida nodded. 'You'll see Mr and Mrs de
Wolff? Shall I say nothing to Gaby until it's all arranged?' She paused. 'I shall have to pack.'

'Yes, of course, I'll go and see them now.'

She went back to the cabin and sat down with a
book. Gaby wasn't sleeping, but she didn't want to
talk either. It was half an hour before Mrs de Wolff
opened the door and came in.

'Well, here's a fine state of affairs!' she exclaimed
angrily. 'All our plans changed just because Gaby
feels a little under the weather! Still, the doctor
knows best, I suppose. My husband's radioed for
rooms for you both at Reid's Hotel and we'll see
you safely there tomorrow before we get back to the
ship.'

Phyllida stared at her. 'But aren't we all going
ashore?'

'Good heavens, no. We've planned it all nicely—
we shall go on to the Canaries and pick you up on

our way back next Saturday. Gaby will be better by
then. We've talked to the doctor, so you have no
need to worry, Miss Cresswell. We feel confident
that you can look after Gaby very well until we return—it's only five days and we simply can't miss
any of this cruise and there's no need for us to do
so. Besides, we've been looking forward to it for
some time.'

She went and peered down at Gaby. 'You do look
a little pale, darling. You'll feel better on dry land,
I expect, and you girls can have a few days' fun on
your own.' She patted Gaby's head and Phyllida saw
the girl wince. 'We'll leave you plenty of spending
money.'

When she had gone Gaby said wearily: 'Mummy
always thinks that if she gives me enough money
everything will be all right.'

'I expect you'll enjoy it just as much as being on
board ship,' said Phyllida soothingly. 'Now, I'm going to pack our things, and suppose we have dinner
here this evening? You choose what you'd like to
eat and get a long night's sleep. Now I'm going to
take these books back to the library.'

She went to see the doctor too, and he wasn't in
the best of tempers. 'I've made it plain to Gaby's
parents that she's extremely ill and possibly heading
for a relapse, and I suggested that you should all fly
back from Madeira tomorrow, but they won't hear

of it—told me that if the specialist considered her fit enough to take a holiday that was good enough for them, that we're probably over-anxious. They agreed readily enough to Gaby going ashore with you—said they'd pick you up at the end of the week. Are you at all worried?'

'I'm in a flat spin,' confided Phyllida. 'Anything could happen, couldn't it? And here we are, thousands of miles away from home and her parents refusing to face up to her being ill. Do you think she'll be all right? I'll take the greatest care of her.'

'If she keeps quiet and with you to look after her she might get over this bad patch, but she really needs to be flown home and taken to hospital, but her parents utterly refuse. They say that this has happened before and she's always got over it.' He sighed. 'At least Mr de Wolff has all the particulars of her case and I've written a covering letter; he's promised to deliver it himself at the hospital and arrange for a doctor to call and see Gaby—probably tomorrow in the evening or the following morning. We shall be back here on Saturday and if Gaby is no better, I'll do my best to persuade her parents to fly her back.'

Phyllida agreed. The doctor had done all he could, she would have the hospital close at hand and a doctor, so perhaps she need not worry too much. Gaby's father had said that these little relapses, as he called them, had occurred before and Gaby had always pulled through with a little extra care. But there were a number of drugs she should be having—perhaps they would have them at the hospital in Funchal. Phyllida didn't quite trust Mr de Wolff's casual view of his daughter's condition, but she had to take his word for it. She packed for them both, saw Gaby into bed for a good night's sleep and went to bed herself.

There was no hitch in the next day's plans. Gaby was cheerful, and after a good night's sleep seemed better. They went ashore just before lunch, went straight to the hotel and lunched there with Gaby's parents before they rejoined the ship. Their goodbyes were brief; they didn't look back as they left the hotel.

Phyllida and Gaby had adjoining rooms overlooking the gardens going down to the sea, with the swimming pools and tennis courts at their edge. They were spacious and airy and Phyllida made her patient comfortable in a long chair on the balcony before unpacking once more and then going to see about meals. When she got back Gaby was sitting up, looking quite animated, watching the guests in the pools. 'I'm going to like it here,' she declared, and looked happy for the first time, 'just with you. We don't need to do anything, do we? I mean, go on excursions or shopping? Daddy gave me some money to hire a car, he said we could tour the island, but I'm not keen, are you?'

'Not a bit,' lied Phyllida. 'I'm all for being lazy. And by the way, Doctor Watts from the ship wrote a note to one of the doctors at the hospital here asking him to pop round and see you this evening or tomorrow, just in case there's anything you need.'

Gaby hunched a shoulder. 'I wish people didn't fuss so. I'm quite all right if only I didn't have this headache.'

'Well, that's why he's coming, I expect; if it's no better he'll be able to prescribe some different tablets. Would you like to stay up here for tea? Or we can have it on the terrace—it looked super and there's a lovely view.'

Gaby settled for the terrace and presently they went downstairs and found seats in a shady corner, and Gaby, Phyllida was pleased to see, enjoyed her tea, talking quite animatedly about her clothes and the boutique they had stopped to look at in the hotel's foyer.

The rest of the day passed pleasantly. They dined at a small table by themselves, but several people around them stopped to speak and Gaby, once more in a happy mood, preened herself in their admiring glances. Phyllida went to bed happier than she had been since the cruise started. Gaby might not be better physically, but she was a whole lot happier. The

thought that it was because her parents weren't there
crossed her mind, but she dismissed that as unlikely.
They gave Gaby everything; she had more clothes
than she ever could wear, lovely jewellery, and
every luxury that money could buy. She was almost
asleep when the notion that Gaby had everything but
real love and interest from her parents came into her
head. She could have wept at the sadness of it.

Gaby felt so well the next morning that she put
on one of her prettiest sun dresses and lounged by
one of the swimming pools while Phyllida swam
around, but as the day became warmer they moved
back to the terrace, ate their lunch there and only
went back to their rooms so that Gaby might rest.
But they went outside again for tea and stayed there
until dinner time, when Gaby changed her dress for
a rather too elaborate silk one, but she looked so
happy that Phyllida told her that she looked a dream
and would turn all heads. Which she did. As they
said goodnight later, Gaby said sleepily: 'It's been
a lovely day—I'd like to stay here, just with you,
Phylly, for ever and ever.'

Phyllida dropped a kiss on the pale cheek and
made some laughing reply before she went to her
own room.

Gaby was awake and sitting up in bed when Phyllida went in the next morning and she left her to
have her breakfast and went downstairs to have her

own, wondering if it would be a good idea to suggest that they might take a taxi to the Country Club and sit there for an hour or two before lunch. She didn't hurry over her meal. Gaby didn't like to be disturbed until she had finished her breakfast; it was almost ten o'clock as she got up from the table. She went back upstairs, pausing to speak to some English guests on their way out. When she knocked on Gaby's door there was no answer; probably she was reading and hadn't heard. Phyllida opened the door.

Gaby wasn't reading. She was lying back in bed, unconscious.

Phyllida drew a startled breath, pulled herself together in seconds and went quickly to the bed. The first thing she did was to press the bell, the second to feel for Gaby's pulse, so faint and threadlike that she had difficulty in finding it. Her breathing was so light and shallow that she had to bend down in order to check it. No one had answered the bell, so she rang again, took the tray off the bed, pulled the pillow into a better position and when there was still no answer to her summons, ran to the door. Something must be done, and fast, if it were to be of any use.

CHAPTER THREE

PHYLLIDA WASN'T a girl to panic, but now she had
to get a tight hold on herself, making her mind work
sensibly when all she wanted to do was scream for
help and leave everything to someone else. This
wasn't hospital, it wasn't even England; she knew
no one, she wasn't even sure where the hospital was.
Gaby was desperately ill—worse than that, Gaby
was going to die. Somehow or other she would have
to get a message to her parents, find a doctor, get
her to hospital. Phyllida took another look at Gaby,
lying so still in her bed, and went downstairs as fast
as she could, running across the foyer to the reception desk.

There was no one there. She banged the bell and
was angry with herself because her hand shook, and
when no one came she couldn't stop herself crying
in a shaky voice: 'Oh, please won't someone come?'

'Will I do?' asked a voice behind her.

It belonged to a very tall, powerfuly built man
with what she immediately decided was a face she
could trust, though at that moment she would have
trusted a snake.

'Yes,' she didn't hesitate. 'I'm looking after a

girl—she's desperately ill and her parents are cruising round the Canaries—I don't know exactly where they are. I need a doctor, now, this instant, and she should be in hospital. She's going to die if something isn't done quickly!'

He put a large firm hand on her arm. 'I'm a doctor, shall I take a look? Do you speak Portuguese?'

'No, but they speak English here, only there isn't anyone.'

'Coffee time. Shall I have a look at this girl? Your patient, is she?'

Phyllida nodded. 'Please. I'll give you an idea...' She started up the stairs fast, talking as she went.

She hadn't doubted that he was a doctor. He examined Gaby with careful speed while Phyllida stood beside him, watching.

There was a great deal of him and he was handsome too, with a patrician nose, a firm mouth and blue eyes beneath lazy lids. His hair was so fair that she wasn't sure if it was grey or not. He straightened up presently and looked at her. 'You're right, I'm afraid—I'll get the hospital, I happen to know someone there. There's nothing more to be done. You know that, don't you?'

'Yes. What shall I do about her parents?'

'When did they go? This girl's been dangerously ill for some time—surely they were told?'

'Yes, oh, yes. But they said that Gaby wanted to

go on this cruise so badly and that's why I'm here, so that I could look after her. She got worse on our way here and the ship's doctor advised us to come ashore with her—he wanted us to fly home, but her parents wouldn't consent. They didn't want her to go to the hospital either…they wouldn't admit that she was ill, I did tell them, but they wouldn't listen. They came ashore with us and then went back on board—and that was the day before yesterday. They told me not to worry about an address if I should need them, they said it wasn't necessary, but I could radio the ship, couldn't I?'

His blue eyes hadn't left her face. 'Don't they love the girl?'

'I—I…it's hard to say; if they do it's not the kind of love most people have for their children—they gave her everything, though. They wanted to get away; her mother hates illness.'

They were in the foyer now and he had a hand on the telephone by the still deserted desk. He lifted the receiver, dialled a number as she spoke and spoke in his turn.

'They'll be here in a few minutes; you'll go with her and stay. I'll get a message to her parents. May I have their name?'

It didn't enter her head to argue with him. 'I'll get her things together and mine too. The name's de Wolff and they're on the *Blenheim*, going to Lanzarote and then Teneriffe and Las Palmas—they're expected back on Saturday.'

'Too late. Now go and get ready. I'll see you later.'

Packing furiously in Gaby's room, one anxious eye on her patient, Phyllida paused for a second. She didn't know the man's name; he might not have been telephoning the hospital, he might just disappear as suddenly as he had appeared; perhaps the ambulance wouldn't come. She shut the case with hands which still shook and then uttered a sigh of relief as she heard steady feet coming down the corridor towards the room.

She should have known better, she chided herself as she got out of the ambulance at the hospital. Her new-found friend was waiting at the entrance with a nurse and doctor and two porters. He wasted no time on greeting her, said merely: 'Follow us,' and led the procession along a corridor, past several wards and into a small room beyond them. Here Gaby was put to bed by Phyllida and the nurse while the two doctors talked together. Once she was asked if she had any notes about her patient and paused to fetch them from her case.

'They were given to me in case the ship's doctor wanted them,' she explained, 'and when he'd read them he pointed out that he hadn't the facilities for Gaby should she become worse. He couldn't understand why she had been allowed on the cruise in the first place. Nothing was said about her being ill when the cruise was booked, he was sure of that. Mrs de Wolff had told me that Gaby was expected to live for another year at least, perhaps longer, but she must have been mistaken.'

The two men nodded and after a minute of reading the big man said: 'She's recently completed her fifth course of chemotheraphy—Daunorubicin and Cytosine.' He glanced at Phyllida. 'Had she started the course of cytoreduction?'

'No, I understood it was to be started when we got back.'

'Well, it's too late to do anything about that now.' He handed back the notes. 'I've sent a radio telegram to the *Blenheim*; we should get an answer very shortly. And now that we know the name of the hospital where she has been treated, we can telephone them.' He paused at the door. 'You'll stay here.' His companion went ahead of him and he turned to say: 'My name is van Sittardt—Pieter van Sittardt.'

'Mine's Phyllida Cresswell.'

'We'll be in the building, ring if you want one of us—we'll be back.'

She was left with the unconscious Gaby and nothing to do but worry as to whether she had neglected to do something which might have saved her patient.

Common sense told her that she hadn't; she had done exactly what she had been told to do. Moreover, she had warned Mr and Mrs de Wolff repeatedly that Gaby wasn't improving. They had taken no notice of her—indeed, she suspected that they had thought that she was being fussy and self-important. Or perhaps they hadn't wanted to know. And they couldn't have delivered the letter from the ship's doctor at the hospital...

Gaby looked beautiful lying there. She might have been asleep, only her pallor was marked and her breathing so light that it was hardly noticeable. It was inconceivable to Phyllida that her parents could have gone off so lightheartedly, knowing, as they surely must have done, that Gaby was very ill indeed. Tidying the already tidy bedcovers, Phyllida wanted to cry.

Gaby died two hours later and it was half an hour after that when the message arrived from her parents.

They would fly back on the following morning.

Phyllida had looked dumbly at Doctor van Sittardt when he had come to tell her. For once her self-possession deserted her and she was uncertain what to do. In hospital there was a fixed procedure, followed to the letter, but here, miles from home with no one to turn to, it was altogether a different matter.

But there was someone to turn to—Doctor van

Sittardt. He suggested that she should return to the hotel and return again after breakfast the next day. 'You've had nothing much to eat, have you? I'll meet you in the bar at half past seven and we'll have dinner together.'

'Yes—well—thank you, but there's…'

'I'll deal with anything that comes up, if you will allow me. There are certain formalities, and her parents aren't here.'

'You're very kind.' Phyllida studied his face and saw its impersonal kindness, and because it was such a relief to let someone else cope, she had agreed, gone back to the hotel, bathed and changed and gone down to the bar to find him waiting for her. She was glad then that she had put on the blue-patterned crêpe and taken pains with her face and hair, for he was wearing a white dinner jacket—and very elegant too, easily the most attractive man there; on any other occasion she would have enjoyed the prospect of an evening in his company, but now she kept remembering Gaby. A shadow crossed her pretty face as he reached her and he said in a friendly, brisk voice: 'Now, Phyllida, no regrets. It was inevitable, and you did everything possible.' He took her arm and found stools at the bar. 'What will you drink?'

He talked about everything under the sun and never once mentioned the day's happenings. Neither did he tell her much about himself; he was staying at the hotel for a day or two and then going to visit friends, Dutch people who lived permanently on Madeira because of the wife's health, but that was all. By the end of the evening Phyllida still didn't know where he lived or anything about him save his name.

Not that there was any need to know, she told herself as she got ready for bed. After tomorrow they weren't likely to see each other again, as she would be going back with the de Wolffs to England and another job. She frowned at her reflection as she sat brushing her hair. Was this perhaps a sign that she should accept Philip after all? If it was she felt remarkably reluctant to take any notice of it. Philip, in the last few hours, had become strangely dim.

She slept soundly, although she hadn't expected to, and went down to breakfast, expecting to see the doctor. There was no sign of him and she ate hurriedly and then made her way in the early morning sunshine to the hospital, and met him at the entrance.

He gave her a businesslike good morning and turned her round smartly. 'I was coming to fetch you from the hotel, but since you're here we may as well go.'

'Go?' she looked at him without understanding.

'To the airport—to meet Gaby's parents.'

'Oh—yes.' She went pink, ashamed that she hadn't thought of that for herself; she should have hired a car to meet them.

The doctor went on placidly: 'I think that perhaps if there are two of us? It's a painful thing to have to do on one's own.'

She gave him a grateful look and got into the rather ramshackle car beside him and he set off without waste of time, travelling east from Funchal to the airport some twenty kilometres away. Half way there Phyllida said: 'I'm scared, having to tell them—you won't leave me, will you?'

His hooded eyes glanced sideways at her pale face. 'No. Tell me something, have the de Wolffs got money?'

She gave him a startled look. 'Well, yes, I think so. He owns several factories and has a big house in the country as well as a London flat. Why do you want to know?'

'It will help when it comes to making arrangements presently.' He overtook a bus with inches to spare. He said quietly: 'Even if I had been a pauper I would have chartered a plane as soon as I'd had that message yesterday.'

'So would I—I expect they feel terrible.'

They didn't have to wait long at the airport. The twice-weekly plane from Las Palmas arrived on time, and within a few minutes the de Wolffs were coming towards them. Mr de Wolff began speaking as soon as he was within a few yards. 'What's all this?' he demanded. 'I hope it's not a wild goose chase. I didn't telephone—no point. Luckily there was a plane leaving this morning, and heaven knows it's been inconvenient.'

And Mrs de Wolff added petulantly: 'Such a rush, and we've had to leave our luggage on board...' She paused and looked at Phyllida. 'What's wrong with Gaby this time?'

'She's dead,' said Phyllida, breaking all the rules of hospital training; bad news should be broken to relations in as gentle a way as possible...but it didn't matter, for the de Wolffs reacted just as she had feared they would. 'Why weren't we told sooner?' and 'I want to know what went wrong!'

It was here that the doctor took over; smoothly but with an edge to his cool professional voice. 'You were told. I sent a radiogram yesterday, asking you to get in touch with the hospital at once. Gaby was desperately ill—I told you that too. And nothing went wrong.' The edge had become a cutting knife. 'She received devoted care from Miss Cresswell and everything that could be done in the hospital was done.'

Phyllida looked at them both, searching for signs of grief, and could find none. Perhaps they were stunned; too shocked to feel anything. She said quietly: 'Doctor van Sittardt most kindly came to my aid yesterday...'

'Surely you knew what to do? We engaged you as a trained nurse.' Mrs de Wolff's voice rose sharply.

'Perhaps I haven't made myself clear,' said the doctor, his voice without expression. 'There was nothing to be done. Gaby was already a very ill girl. You knew that?'

Mrs de Wolff threw him an angry glance. 'Well, of course—the doctors told us she would die, but not as soon as this.'

'If she had stayed in hospital, or even quietly at home,' observed the doctor, carefully noncommittal, 'her life might have been prolonged for a short time.'

'We needed a break, we'd already booked on this cruise.' Mr de Wolff answered for his wife. 'We thought it would do her good, make her forget she was sickly.' He looked away from the doctor's stare and added uncomfortably: 'It isn't as though she were our own daughter. We adopted her when she was a baby—she was a gay little thing when she was a child, but she grew up so quiet and dull.'

The doctor didn't reply to this, neither did Phyllida, and after a moment Mr de Wolff said irritably: 'Well, we'd better go to the hospital, I suppose.'

He and his wife got into the back of the car and

Phyllida settled herself beside the doctor, trying not to hear Mrs de Wolff grumbling behind her. 'I shall have to have this dress cleaned,' she complained, 'this is a dreadful car.' And then: 'I suppose we'll have to arrange to have Gaby taken back home, otherwise people might think it strange.'

Phyllida sat very upright, staring before her, her eyes wide so that she might stop her tears. Not that it helped; they tumbled silently down her cheeks and she wiped them away with a finger, stealing a glance at her companion to make sure that he hadn't noticed. He was staring ahead too, driving a little too fast, his mouth grim. He hadn't seen, she thought with relief, then went a slow red as his hand, large and cool, came down on hers and gave it a comforting squeeze. But he didn't look at her.

She wondered afterwards how she had got through that morning. Sorrow, regret, shock she could have coped with, but neither of the de Wolffs needed sympathy. Reluctantly they had conceded, in the face of the doctor's firm statement, that Phyllida had done all that she had been able to do, but they expressed no gratitude, only plunged briskly into the problems facing them, and when she asked them when she would be returning to England they told her that they would all fly back together in a few days' time, so that when Doctor Sittardt wanted to know if her future was settled, she was able to tell him that she would be leaving with the de Wolffs.

She helped Mrs de Wolff pack up Gaby's things after breakfast the next morning while Mr de Wolff was at the airport, making final arrangements, and when Mrs de Wolff suggested quite kindly that she might like to have a swim in the hotel pool before lunch, she went gladly, quite touched by her employer's consideration.

The water was warm and the sun shone. Phyllida swam lazily for a while, lay in the hot sunshine for a while and then went to dress ready for lunch. From her bedroom window she saw the *Blenheim* lying on the other side of the harbour; she would be sailing shortly and they should all have been on board by now, going home. Phyllida sighed, slipped into a cotton dress, brushed her hair smooth and went downstairs. Mrs de Wolff had told her to wait for them in the bar, and she chose a table in a corner and found herself wishing that the doctor had been there to keep her company. She hadn't seen him since they had left the hospital on the previous day and by now he would be with his friends. She occupied her time thinking about him because it wouldn't help anyone to think about Gaby and it was hard not to do that when she was on her own. It surprised her presently to find that she had been there for more than half an hour and, vaguely un-

easy, she asked one of the barmen if there was a
message for her and then, at his positive 'No', went
to the reception desk and asked the same question.

She was surprised when she was handed a note,
but not unduly alarmed. Something must have pre-
vented Mr de Wolff from returning from the airport
and probably his wife had gone out there to meet
him. She opened the envelope and wandered out on
to the terrace to read her letter. It was very hot now
and the sea was a deep blue under the cloudless sky.
The *Blenheim*, she noticed idly, was edging out of
the harbour.

The letter was brief but its message was clear
enough; the de Wolffs, their arrangements made at
the airport concerning Gaby, had decided to sail
home on the *Blenheim*. They were sure that Miss
Cresswell would understand and she could follow in
her own good time, taking whichever route she preferred. A cheque covering her fees was awaiting her
at the Fred Olsen offices in the town.

Phyllida sat down abruptly on a stone bench and
reread the letter. No mention was made of a return
ticket. She supposed they had forgotten it; they must
have also forgotten that there wouldn't be another
boat for a week, and although there were two flights
a day to England they went via Lisbon and would
doubtless cost a good deal of money. And she hadn't
a great deal of that with her; enough to buy presents

and small necessities for herself, but she very much doubted if that and the cheque they had left for her would be enough to get her back home. And what about the hotel bill?

All thought of lunch escaped her. She went back to the reception desk and asked about the bill and heaved a sigh of relief to find that it had been paid, but only until the following day. She told the clerk that she would be leaving then and went to get her handbag. She was halfway down the hill to the town when she remembered that it was Saturday and the shipping office would be closed. The only thing to do would be to visit the Tourist Office and find out about hotels.

And when she got there it was to discover that they had shut for the afternoon siesta. At a loss, Phyllida wandered down the Avenida Arriaga and into the Jardim de Sao Francisco and sat down under the trees. There weren't many people about in the heat of the day although there was plenty of traffic, providing a background for her thoughts.

Good sense was taking over from the feeling of panic she had been struggling to ignore. It should be easy enough to find a small, cheap hotel for a couple of nights and surely her money would stretch to a flight home on Monday—perhaps the night flights were cheaper if she could get on one. And once she was back in London everything would be all right. She could cash a cheque at the bank, tele-phone home; go home. She closed her eyes and leaned back against a juniper tree.

'They were a little concerned about you at the hotel,' remarked Doctor van Sittardt quietly as he sat down beside her. He put out a hand and pushed her gently back as she started up. 'You left rather suddenly without your lunch.' He glanced at her. 'The clerk mentioned a letter.'

He obviously expected an answer and Phyllida realised that he was exactly what she needed—vast and calm and reassuring. She managed the shadow of a smile, dug into her handbag and handed him Mrs de Wolff's note. 'I always thought,' she ob-served in a small voice, 'that I was a capable person, able to cope with things when they went wrong, but it seems I'm not. I rushed straight out of the hotel to get a cheaper hotel and book a flight back to England on Monday, but of course everything's closed for the weekend or until four o'clock. So I thought I'd come here and think things out.'

He had been reading while she spoke, now he glanced up, his blue eyes studying her steadily from under their heavy lids. 'I suspected something like this would happen; if they could dismiss Gaby's death so easily they weren't likely to treat you any differently. I should have warned you, but as you say, you are a capable girl, quite able to cope.'

Phyllida nodded, her teeth clamped together to stop the trembling of her mouth. He thought her able to take care of herself and was doubtless thankful that he wouldn't have to put himself out any more on her account. All right, she would look capable even if it killed her!

'Well now,' went on her companion blandly, 'shall we go and have lunch, or would you like a good howl first? It's very pleasant here and not many people about, and I'll lend you my shoulder.'

Phyllida unclenched her teeth and let out a tiny wail. 'Oh, however did you guess? And you've just said I'm so capable!' She made herself sit up straight. 'But I'm all right now, really I am—it was having a surprise… Do please go and have your own lunch, I'm not hungry.'

He said patiently: 'I guessed because I've sisters of my own to plague me, and however capable you are, you have to let go sometimes. A drink is what you need, and a meal. You can weep to your heart's content afterwards if you still want to.'

He swept her to her feet and walked her briskly, despite the heat, back towards the heart of the city. Down a narrow side street he stopped in front of a small restaurant, its tables spilling out on to the pavement, its interior dim and cool. He must have been known there, for they were given a table in a corner by an open window and offered a menu.

'Sercial, I think, before we eat,' said the doctor, glancing at her still pale face. 'It's very dry but splendid before a meal. We'll have Malmsey afterwards. This is a fish restaurant, but if you don't like fish, there's chicken or omelettes.'

'I like fish.' Phyllida took a gulp of her Madeira.

'Good. We'll have *bifes de atum*—that's tuna steaks—and sweet potatoes in fritters and *pudim Mareira* to follow.'

'What's that?'

'A caramel flan with Madeira sauce. Very nice.'

She took another sip and began to feel better. 'You know Madeira well?'

'I come here from time to time.' And that was all he had to say, so that to break the silence she said awkwardly:

'It looks very beautiful. I must try and come back one day and explore.'

He didn't answer at once; the fish had come and she eyed it with pleasure, her appetite sharpened. It wasn't until they had made inroads into the delicious food that he spoke. 'How much money have you?'

She paused, her fork half way to her mouth. 'Oh, enough, I think. I'll find a small hotel until Monday and book a flight home then.'

'Do you know how much the fare is?' He mentioned a sum which made her catch her breath.

'That's the return, I expect,' she said hopefully.

'No, single. I think you should stay with my friends until the next ship calls on its way back to England.'

'Oh, but I couldn't—that's a week…besides, the fare…'

'I'll telephone their head office. The de Wolffs paid for your round trip, didn't they? So unless they've claimed a refund, your passage is already paid.'

Relief almost choked her. 'Oh, I hadn't thought of that. I can stay here until it comes—I'm bound to find an hotel.'

He finished his fish and leaned back in his chair. 'Phyllida, if you were me and I were you, would you offer to help me? And expect me to accept?'

'Of course I would!' She had spoken before thinking and he smiled.

'Well, that's all I'm doing. My friends will love to have you; Metha is rather crippled with arthritis and will enjoy your company.'

'Yes, but I can't…'

'We'll go back to the hotel presently and pick up your things and I'll drive you out there. I'll give them a ring while you're packing.'

She said weakly: 'But supposing they don't want me to stay? They don't know me.'

'How could they when they haven't met you?' he asked reasonably. 'Ah, here is our Madeira pudding—they do it very well here. There are some excellent restaurants in Funchal and quite a few scattered round the island. We must take you to some of them before you go back.'

They had almost finished their pudding when he asked: 'Do you want to telephone your family?'

She swallowed the last delicious morsel. 'Well, they're rather—I think they might worry; I thought a letter. If I send it today?'

He shook his head. 'No good, the *Blenheim* will get there long before the letter. Were you going straight home?'

'Yes.'

'Then telephone. You could say that plans have been changed and you'll be back a week later.'

The waiter brought two glasses of Malmsey and the doctor ordered coffee. Phyllida, who could think of no reason for disputing his suggestion, agreed.

They went unhurriedly back to the hotel presently, and she went up to her room to pack her things, leaving the doctor to tell the receptionist and telephone his friends. When she went down half an hour later, he was sitting on the terrace, his feet on a chair, reading an old copy of the *Telegraph*. There was a tall glass at his elbow, half full, and as he got to his feet he waved to a waiter and ordered her a drink. 'I'm drinking lager, but I've ordered you a lemonade and lime. Will that do?'

'Yes, thank you.' She sat down opposite him and he lounged back in his chair again.

'The de Meesters—my friends—are delighted to have you for as long as you like to stay. They want us up there for tea.'

'Do they live far away?' she asked.

He waved vaguely towards the mountains which swept up and away behind the town. 'No—in a village about five kilometres to the north—Monte. It used to be the island's capital and it's full of lovely old houses. There's a magnificent church too.'

He finished his drink and stretched out again, and Phyllida had the impression that if she hadn't been there he would have closed his eyes and had a nap. She sipped her own drink, relaxing under his casual calm, knowing that he didn't expect her to make conversation. When she had finished he sat up, all at once brisk. 'Right, did someone bring down your luggage?'

She nodded. 'Yes, it's at reception.' She hesitated. 'You've been very kind, Doctor van Sittardt.'

He smiled, a warm slow smile that transformed his rather austere good looks and made her feel safe and secure. 'The name's Pieter.' He got to his feet and stretched out a hand and pulled her out of her chair. 'Let's go and see if that car will start.'

The little car was certainly shabby, but there was nothing wrong with its engine. They went slowly through the town and then into the Rua 31 de Janeiro, and presently turned right into the Rua do Til. The drive might have been only five kilometres, but it was uphill all the way, and Phyllida, who had seen nothing of the island, was enchanted by the scenery as they climbed steadily up into the mountains. The doctor slowed down from time to time so that she could take it all in—the towering grey heights, the little green meadows tucked between them, with eucalyptus, mimosa and juniper trees, the small red-tiled houses, and from time to time a luxurious modern villa. He pointed Monte out to her before they reached it, to one side of the road, cloud hanging above it, its houses, and church clinging to the summit. The houses on its outskirts were modern, white-walled and red-tiled like the farms and each with its trailing vines and bougainvillea, with wisteria and the blue of the jacaranda trees adding splashes of bright colour. But once in the centre of the small place, they were back in the eighteenth century, for its square was lined with balconied houses of great age, overshadowd by the church and the mountains around them. The doctor turned the car down a narrow side street and then turned again through a wide arched gateway leading to a paved courtyard, enclosed on three sides by grey stone walls pierced by high narrow windows and with a massive door in its centre.

He stopped the car and leaned across Phyllida to open her door. 'We're here, and in case you find it rather forbidding, it's much nicer inside.'

The door was opened before they reached it by a small dark woman who smiled gravely at them and led the way across a wide dim hall to a door at one side. She flung this open, said something to whoever was inside, and stood back to let them pass.

The room was dim too with dark panelled walls and a plain white ceiling. The floor was tiled and covered by thin rugs in lovely colours and the furniture was dark and massive. There were two people in the room, a man and a woman, and the man got up at once and came towards them, his hand held out.

'Welcome, Miss Cresswell. You cannot know how glad we are to have you as our guest.' He engulfed her hand in his and beamed down at her. He was almost as tall as Pieter van Sittardt but inclined to stoutness, with a pleasant rugged face and fair hair already receding from a high forehead. 'You will forgive my wife if she doesn't get up.' He held her hand still and led her across the room to where a youngish woman was sitting in a high-backed chair. She was still very pretty with fair hair and dark eyes and she was dressed with great elegance. Only her crippled hands gave away the fact that she was an invalid. But that was forgotten when she spoke.

'I shall not call you Miss Cresswell,' she declared in a pretty voice. 'Phyllida is such a pretty name—mine's Metha,' she nodded towards her husband, 'and he is Hans. It is lovely to have you and I am so happy—these two talk about their work all the time and do not care for clothes.' She lifted a face to Pieter who bent to kiss her cheek.

'I should hope not indeed,' he declared, 'but you and Phyllida can talk to your hearts' content. I expect you miss the children.'

Metha nodded. 'Oh yes, very much—but now I have Phyllida and shall speak English all the time so that I will be occupied all the time and be happy.'

She smiled at Phyllida. 'You do not speak Portuguese, or Dutch?' and went on in a satisfied voice: 'No? That is splendid for me, for I shall improve my English and teach you a little besides.'

The solemn-faced woman brought in tea then, tea in a pot, Phyllida saw with pleasure, and plenty of milk in a jug, as well as a plate of little cakes and sugary biscuits. 'We like our tea,' explained Metha, 'it is for us a pleasant hour of the day, just to sit and talk.'

And very pleasant it was, Phyllida agreed silently, and how very at home Pieter looked, stretched out in one of the heavy tapestry-covered armchairs. It

was evident that he was a friend of long standing
but all the same, they all took care to include her in
their talk, touching lightly on her reason for being
there and then ignoring it to talk about Madeira and
their life there.

Metha did most of the talking in her pretty En-
glish with her husband joining in frequently, only
Pieter van Sittardt remained almost silent, looking,
Phyllida decided, almost too lazy to open his mouth.

The pleasant little meal came to its leisurely end
and Phyllida was taken upstairs by the solemn
woman, who led the way along a corridor to a room
at the back of the house, with a balcony overlooking
a small paved yard with a fountain in its centre.
Phyllida heaved a sigh of pure pleasure at the sight
of it; things could have been so much worse—a
small hotel and the worry of wondering if her money
would hold out and business of getting a ticket for
home. She would have to see about that on Monday
morning; she couldn't impose on her new friends,
whatever the doctor had said.

She unpacked and hung her things away, took a
shower, changed her dress and went downstairs
again.

CHAPTER FOUR

THERE WAS ONLY one occupant of the sitting room as she entered, the doctor, lounging back in a great armchair, his enormous feet on a convenient coffee table. He appeared to be asleep, but he wasn't, for he was on his feet before she had taken two steps into the room.

'Hullo,' he smiled disarmingly at her, 'the others will be down directly. Metha said I was to give you a drink.' He pulled forward a chair and she sat down. 'Have something long and cool; they dine rather later than we do at home.'

'Thank you.' Phyllida went on hurriedly: 'I've not had the chance to thank you properly for everything you've done—you've been simply super.'

'I think that we agreed that you would have done the same for me?' He dismissed her thanks with casual ease. 'Now, this drink—how about a Pimms with not too much gin?'

He mixed the drink, handed it to her, poured himself a whisky and sat down again. 'Metha thinks it might be fun if we drove round a bit tomorrow and showed you the sights. She wants you to see Cabo Girao—that's a very high sea cliff to the west of

Funchal. It's a pretty drive there and afterwards we might go on to Ribeira Brava, it won't be crowded yet—we might even swim, but Metha's a bit shy of going into the water if there's anyone about. Hans carries her in; he swims on his back and takes her with him.'

'She's so pretty and young.' Phyllida's eyes searched her companion's face. 'Isn't there anything to be done?'

'Not much, I'm afraid. She had acute rheumatoid arthritis after the second child was born; she doesn't have much pain now, but it's left her with limited movement. She's a wonderful person, never complains and always looks so serene and marvellously turned out. She and Hans have the kind of marriage one hopes for and seldom achieves.'

'Are you married?'

He smiled slowly. 'No, I've always considered myself to be a dedicated bachelor. However, I think it very likely that I shall change my mind; there's something very appealing about a wife and children to comfort my old age.'

She looked a question, not quite daring to ask it.

'And I'm thirty-nine.' He glanced at her from under heavy lids. 'You, Phyllida? Are you married, divorced, engaged or having what I believe is called a close relationship with some lucky man?'

'Oh, I don't believe in that,' declared Phyllida.

Her blue eyes met his candidly. 'And I'm not married or divorced.' She added after a pause: 'Nor engaged.'

'Thinking about it?' he asked lazily.

She shook her head. 'Not any more—it was just—
well, we sort of slid into supposing that we might
get married later on and then I discovered that I
didn't love him at all, only liked him very much.'

'Now it's so often the other way round with me,'
murmured the doctor. 'I fall in love with a girl and
then discover that I don't like her.'

She wondered what kind of girls he fell in love
with and then told herself that it was none of her
business. All the same she was trying to think of a
way of putting a tactful question or two when Metha
and Hans came in. Metha was walking with two
sticks, but she looked so pretty and happy that it
went almost unnoticed; besides, she broke into
lively chatter as soon as she was in the room.

'We'll have dinner in half an hour and then have
coffee on the terrace,' she declared happily. 'It's
such a beautiful evening and the sunset is always a
delight. Phyllida, come over here and sit with me
and tell me where you bought that pretty dress.
There are one or two good shops here, but not very
much choice. Twice a year we go to Holland for a
visit and I do as much shopping as I can while we're
there, but you know what men are; you put on a hat

and they say: "that's fine, dear", and there you are saddled with something hideous, suitable for an aunt!'

They all laughed and Phyllida looked across at the doctor and found him staring at her, his eyes half shut, as usual. She pinkened faintly; he would think her horribly unfeeling to be enjoying herself so much, with Gaby...

He had read her expression unerringly. 'Now, Phyllida!' He shook his head at her and smiled so kindly that she had the sudden urge to run across the room and bury her face in his shoulder and howl her eyes out. But she wasn't given the chance; he went on: 'Why don't you two girls do some shopping tomorrow afternoon? We could go to Cabo Girao in the morning, lunch at Camara de Lobos at that nice place—the Riba Mar, isn't it?—and drop you both off at that boutique you go to in Funchal, Metha. Come to that, we'll park the car and come with you.' He grinned at Phyllida. 'I might even buy you a hat.'

The dinner was delicious, although Phyllida wasn't sure what they ate most of the time, and she was too shy to ask. The two men ate hugely, leaving most of the talking to the two girls and keeping their glasses filled with a light table wine which was presently replaced by Malmsey which they drank with their coffee.

It was still warm on the terrace and the view over the mountains and down towards Funchal and the sea was breathtakingly lovely in the late evening. The talk was quiet now, an effortless flow which Phyllida found very soothing. Presently the doctor got up and came over to where she was sitting. 'Come to the end of the terrace,' he suggested, 'we can see the sunset from there and with any luck you'll see the green flash.'

She got up willingly. 'What's that?'

He shrugged huge shoulders. 'I'm not sure—it sometimes follows a Madeira sunset.'

The back of the house overlooked a sloping garden which in turn led to a banana plantation, sweeping down to the ravine far below, and on the other side the mountains towered, but the valley between allowed them a clear view of the sun, setting in a blaze of colour. It was all so beautiful and Phyllida, looking at it, found to her horror that she was on the verge of tears. She muttered: 'Oh, poor Gaby, not to be able to see all this.'

A great arm was flung across her shoulders. 'There's no one but us,' he told her gently. 'Have your cry, my dear, you'll feel better for it.'

She sucked in her breath like a little girl. 'It's all such a waste,' she stopped to sniff, fighting the tears still, 'and I can't see why.'

'My dear child, I say that every day in my work,

but I don't expect to be given the answer.' He turned her round so that her head rested comfortably on his chest and stood patiently while she sobbed, and presently he said: 'Feel better? Turn round, the sun's just going down.'

They stood together, his arm still round her, and watched the sky deepen its colour, and then as the sun sank from sight, they saw the green flash.

'That's something you can tell your friends about when you get back to the hospital.' He had fished a handkerchief from a pocket and handed it to her and she was mopping her face.

'I'm not going back. I—I left St Michael's just before I came on this trip.'

'Want to talk about it?' His casual voice invited confidence.

She hadn't realised how much she had wanted to talk to someone; it all came tumbling out and when she had finished: 'And the awful thing is I'm sure— at least, I'm not sure, but I think I may have made a frightful mistake; Philip's so—so safe.' She added quickly: 'I'm boring you.'

'No, you're not, and if I might offer my opinion for what it's worth; the frightful mistake would be if you were to marry Philip.'

He looked down at her thoughtfully, his eyes almost hidden under their lids. 'I think you're a girl who needs to marry for love and nothing else—you don't have any doubts if you love someone, you know.'

'I know you're right. I'm just being cowardly about looking for another job—all those forms to fill in and the interviews and then getting to know everyone.'

'In your English you say: "Don't cross your bridges until you come to them". Such a wise piece of advice. Why do you not take a holiday?' He gave her shoulder a brotherly pat. 'You have a family?'

She found herself telling him about her home, her mother and father and Willy who was going to be a doctor like his father, and Dick who was in his last year at a veterinary college and Beryl, just twenty, who was at Bristol University. 'I think I will have a holiday,' she finished, 'just for a couple of weeks while I make up my mind where I want to go.'

'A splendid idea. And now as to the immediate future. I find that I shall be going back with the next ship too; we shall be fellow passengers, and in the meantime we may as well enjoy ourselves here. Metha and Hans love having guests and I know that she longs for more female company at times. Besides, we're an excellent excuse for sightseeing—she has a passion for picnics, too. When the children are on holiday she can arrange one every day, but they're in Holland and Hans is away all day she's very much alone. He's on holiday at the moment because I'm here.'

'It sounds wonderful, but are you sure—I mean, I just can't stay here for a week...'

'Metha would be heartbroken if you didn't. Besides, with you here, we can slope off on our own.'

Phyllida laughed a little. 'Of course, if you put it like that, I haven't any choice, have I?'

'None whatever.' He turned her round and deliberately studied her face in the twilight. 'Tears all gone? Good, we'll join the others, shall we? They'll want to make plans for tomorrow.'

They took her to Cabo Girao the following day, driving back to Funchal and along the coast road, climbing all the way, with the sea below on one side, and a scattering of villages on the other. There were flowers everywhere; nasturtiums, wisteria and echium jostled for a place, with jacaranda trees making great splashes of colour next the bougainvillea, and every wayside cottage and villa had a garden crowded with every sort of flower. Phyllida craned her pretty neck in her efforts to see everything which was being pointed out to her, sitting beside Pieter who was driving his friend's Mercedes, with Hans and Metha in the back.

'There's a dragon tree!' exclaimed Metha, and Pieter slowed the car so that Phyllida should get a good view of it before racing on, still climbing.

The cliff, when they reached it, was spectacular, but she was glad of Pieter's arm round her shoulders as they hung over the rail to stare down to the sea far below, and she was secretly relieved when they rejoined Metha in the car and drove down to Camara de Lobo, where they had lunch, and then, while Hans and Metha stayed on the restaurant's terrace, the doctor took Phyllida for a stroll on the beach to get a closer look at the gaily painted boats. Phyllida scuffed her sandalled feet happily in the shingle and wished the day would last for ever; it didn't seem possible that she had known her companion for such a short time; he was like an old friend, easygoing, goodnaturedly answering her questions, treating her like a sister. She stopped to examine a shell and wondered why she didn't really want him to treat her with such offhand ease. Yet, after all, they were only acquaintances, brought together by circumstances, and once she was back in England she wouldn't see him any more. She stole a look at him, meandering along beside her. He was already deeply tanned, so that his hair looked like silvered straw, and his eyes, when he bothered to lift the lids, were a quite startling blue. His face seemed haughty in repose, but that was because his nose was large and arrogant and his mouth firm. He was indeed a handsome man. He looked sideways at her, catching her unawares, and she went red and looked away quickly. But when she made to walk a little apart from him he caught her hand and didn't let it go. 'Enjoying yourself?' he wanted to know.

'Oh, yes, it's super. I didn't expect to see anything of Madeira, you know.'

'We'll take the toboggan ride tomorrow—that's something everyone does when they come here. We'll go early before the tourists arrive.' He stopped to look at her. 'Can you swim?'

'Not very well, but I like it.'

'Good. We'll go to Ponta de Sao Lourenço, that's the only sandy beach there is. We can take Metha, of course, because there'll be no one much there and she can go in the water. We'll go over the Poiso pass and through Santo da Serra; it's a pretty run, you'll like it.'

'It sounds lovely, but I do have to go to the shipping office and collect my cheque and see about going back.'

'I hadn't forgotten. You and Metha can spend ten minutes in a boutique—it'll be open—and Hans and I will go and get your money and see about a sailing.'

'I can't bother you...'

'I'm not in the least bothered, I have to get a passage for myself too.'

'Oh, yes—of course.' She gave her hand a little tug and his grip tightened ever so gently.

'You haven't been around much, have you?' His voice was as gentle as his fingers.

She knew what he meant. 'No, I suppose not, there's not a lot of time for a social life—one comes off duty tired and only longing to kick off one's shoes and make a pot of tea. I used to go out more often before I met Philip.'

'You didn't go out with him?' He sounded surprised.

'Well, yes, of course—I meant we didn't go dancing or to shows or anything like that, just to a restaurant for supper or to his brother's house.'

There was no expression on her companion's face. 'It sounds cosy.' His voice was dry and she gave another tug at her hand.

'No, leave it where it is. You're a pretty girl, Phyllida, you should have your chance to play the field, meet people, and by that I mean men of your own age. Who knows if you go into the wide world and fall in and out of love a few times, you may go back to your Philip after all.'

She didn't fancy the idea somehow. Philip seemed far away, belonging to another world. The thought crossed her mind that it might be fun to fall in love with Pieter. Just a little, of course; he was a very attractive man and doubtless he had a girl at home. It was a pity that she didn't know him well enough to ask him; it struck her that he had asked her a great many more questions than she had done of him. Not that it mattered, he was a chance encounter...

She reminded herself of that several times during the day; just to be on the safe side, but it was a little difficult. Hans was a chance encounter too, but with him it didn't seem at all the same.

But she enjoyed herself, spending a pleasant half hour with Metha in the boutique, looking at bright cotton dresses and beautifully cut bikinis. She didn't dare buy anything, though.

The men came back presently and Pieter handed her an envelope. 'If you sign the cheque, I'll go across to the bank and get it cashed,' he told her. 'Have you any traveller's cheques with you?'

'No—they said I wouldn't need any money because they would be paying me. I've a few pounds, though, as well as some money I brought along just in case—it's not much, though.'

She opened the envelope. The cheque was for the exact number of days she had worked for the de Wolffs. No one had thought of her expenses, but all the same there would be enough to get her home now provided she didn't spend more than a pound or two in Madeira. She slid the cheque back into the envelope and Pieter, who had been talking to the others, turned round. 'You won't need any money for your fare,' he told her casually. 'They checked

with their head office and you've been given a
ticket—on the boat deck, a single cabin. The ship
sails at two o'clock on Saturday.'

'And now you don't need to save your money,'
interpolated Metha, 'we shall go right back into the
boutique and you shall buy that Indian cotton sun-
dress—and I think I shall buy one too.' She beamed
at the men. 'And you, my dears, may come with us.'

They went in together and the shop owner surged
forward, produced a chair for Metha and whisked
Phyllida away with an armful of dresses over her
arm. The one she had liked, a vivid blue tied carelessly on the shoulders and with a deep scooped out
neckline, was a perfect fit. Urged by the shop lady,
she went back into the shop from the tiny fitting
room and showed herself to the three of them.
'Beautiful,' said Metha at once. 'Smashing,' declared Hans, who prided himself on his up-to-date
English, and: 'You'll need a bikini to go underneath
that,' observed Pieter lazily.

So she bought a bikini too and for good measure
a wide-brimmed straw hat, and while she was trying
it on, the doctor, who had been prowling round on
his own, came back with a silk dress flung over his
arm. It was a delicate green patterned with the
faintest of pinks.

'Try that on too,' he begged her. 'We're going
dancing tomorrow.'

Which seemed a good enough reason for doing just that, and finding it to be a perfect fit, buying it too.

They spent the evening at the de Meesters' house and after dinner the doctor took Phyllida for a stroll round the little town and then up the path through the park to the church, and as they walked round its dim coolness he told her about Nossa Senhora do Monte, whose bejewelled statue held pride of place on the high altar.

'Rather lovely, isn't she?' he said very quietly. 'I'm not a Catholic myself, but she stands for a great deal to many people living on the island—they come each year, thousands of them, to see Our Lady of the Mountain.'

They strolled back presently through the cool evening and then once more indoors, spent the rest of the evening playing a noisy game of Canasta.

They went swimming the next day, but only after the doctor had kept his promise to Phyllida and taken her on the toboggan ride. He drove her away from Monte, up into the hills beyond, with Hans beside them, so that he could drive the car back to his house. It was still early and there weren't many people about. Leaving Hans and the car they took a narrow path which brought them out on to a cobbled lane where the toboggans were waiting, each with two men, dressed in their uniform of white suits and straw hats.

The journey took perhaps five minutes, the toboggan sliding at speed over the ridged cobbles, guided by the two men. Phyllida found it a bit alarming, especially on the frequent hairpin-bends, but it was fun too and she had Pieter to hang on to. 'You've done it before,' she gasped, half way down.

'Lord, yes—half a dozen times.' He didn't add with a girl, but she guessed that. 'Enjoying it?'

She nodded, her silky hair flying round her head, her eyes sparkling like a child's. 'But I'd hate to do it on my own.'

'I don't think there's any fear of that.'

The ride ended by the church they had visited on the previous evening, and tourists were already going in and out of its doors, stopping to examine and buy the embroidered handkerchiefs laid out neatly on large trays carried by the local man. But they didn't stop, going down the path again and back into the town and the de Meesters' house.

'Just time to put on the sun-dress,' remarked the doctor as they went inside, 'and don't forget the bikini!'

It was an hilarious day. Phyllida, lying awake at the end of it, went carefully over every minute of it. Pieter had driven the car, taking them up into the mountains through the kind of scenery she thought

she would never see again, over the Poiso Pass,
through the charming countryside past the golf
course, tucked away on a small plateau and, she had
considered, a bit inaccessible, and then on to Canical
which she hadn't much cared for; it was dominated
by a whale oil factory and looked forlorn. It was
from here that they had to walk; not far, as it happened, for Pieter took the car to the very edge of
the sand dunes which led to the beach. They had a
light wheelchair with them for Metha and Pieter carried the picnic basket and no one hurried. The beach
was almost deserted and the men went back to the
car for airbeds, a huge sun umbrella, a basket full
of tins of beer and lemonade and armfuls of cush-
ions. Phyllida, remembering picnics at home—pot-
ted meat sandwiches and a thermos—got quite gog-
gle-eyed at the lavishness of the food; delicate little
sandwiches, potato fritters, cold, accompanying *es-
pada* fish, cold chicken, tomato salad—there was no
end. She had eaten a bit of everything with a splendid appetite and washed it down with lemonade.
And it hadn't been hot, there had been a breeze from
the sea and the water had been surprisingly cool.
She had taken off the sun-dress rather shyly because
there really hadn't been much of the bikini, but the
doctor had barely glanced at her, and once in the
water she had forgotten her shyness and after a few
minutes close to the beach, she had struck out

bravely, heading out to sea. She'd heard Metha laughing as Hans towed her through the water; Pieter she hadn't seen, not until he appeared beside her, swimming with no effort at all.

'They catch whales here,' he told her.

Phyllida, the kind of swimmer to sink like a stone at the least alarm, let out a small scream, swallowed a good deal of water and gurgled so alarmingly that the doctor flipped her over on to her back and slid an arm beneath her. 'When I said here,' he had pointed out unhurriedly, 'I meant some miles out to sea.'

He was paddling alongside her, looking at the sky. 'If you've finished spluttering, let's go back. Do you think you're strong enough to hold Metha up on one side, I'll hang on to the other. Then Hans can go for a swim.'

They had done that, with Metha, her thin arms on their shoulders, between them. It hadn't been quite like swimming, but it was the next best thing, and no one, unless they had looked very closely, would have known the difference; the water helped, of course, allowing her more movement, and Pieter acted just as though she were doing it all by herself. He was nice, thought Phyllida sleepily, and he had been even nicer that evening. True to his promise he had taken her down to Funchal after dinner, to the Hotel Savoy, where they had danced, watched the folk dancing and then danced again, and on the way back to Monte, at two o'clock in the morning, they had stopped at a noisy, dimly lit street café and had coffee and brandy.

Monte's narrow streets and old houses had been dark. The doctor stopped the car soundlessly and got out to open her door and then the house door. There was a lamp burning in the hall and the old house had seemed not quite real in the utter silence. She had thanked him for a lovely evening and wished him goodnight, and for answer he had caught her arm and walked her through the house to the terrace beyond. 'You can't go to bed before you've seen the view,' he had told her, and taken her to the very end of it.

It wasn't quite time for the dawn, but the sky to the east was already paling, and turning at the touch of his hand she had seen the dark outline of the mountains and the even darker ravines and beyond them the lights still burning in the outskirts of Funchal.

'All the years I've wasted in London,' she had said, talking to herself.

'Not wasted—and not so many—you can always make up for lost time.'

She had said: 'I'm not likely to come here again—not for a long time.' She didn't suppose that he had to worry overmuch about money and although she wasn't exactly poor, her salary hardly ran to the kind of holiday she was enjoying now. She turned away and gone back indoors and he had followed her, locking the glass doors after him. In the hall, at the foot of the stairs, she had said again: 'Thank you, Pieter,' and would have added a few conventional remarks to round off their evening, but she didn't have the chance. He had kissed her then—she turned over in bed and thumped her pillows, remembering it. She had been silly to think that it might be fun to fall a little in love with him. It wouldn't be fun at all, it would be disaster—a dead end affair with him bidding her a cheerful goodbye when they got to London, forgetting her the moment her back was turned. It had been an unexpected holiday, she reminded herself, and as so often happened on holiday, one met someone one rather liked and enjoyed a casual, short-lived friendship. She closed her eyes on this sensible thought; she was almost asleep when she remembered that Pieter had told her that she looked beautiful in the new dress.

After that the days flashed by, filled by picnics in beautiful remote spots and a drive to Ponta Delgada on the north coast, over the Eucumeada Pass, where they had stopped so that Phyllida might feast her eyes on the magnificent view from its top, and they had lunched at the hotel close by before driving on through the mountains. She would have liked to have stopped again, there was so much to see, but as Pieter explained, the roads were winding and precipitous and it wasn't always possible. Not that he seemed to mind the hazards; he drove with nonchalant ease whether they were going uphill, downhill or round hairpin bends which made her glad she wasn't driving. And that evening they had gone dancing again, only this time he didn't kiss her goodnight.

Saturday came too soon, she bade Metha and Hans goodbye with real regret for it seemed as though they had been lifelong friends, and then stood aside while the doctor made his own farewells, brief and cheerful, before he took her arm and hurried her on board.

Their cabins were next door to each other and very much to her taste, roomy and comfortable and spotlessly clean. She would unpack at once, she decided, but she had scarcely opened her overnight bag before the doctor thumped on her door. 'They'll wait on the quay until we leave,' he explained. 'We'd better go on deck.'

So she went with him, to hang over the rail and shout to Metha and watch the last-minute buying and selling going on round the little stalls set up alongside the ship, while Pieter lounged beside her, not saying much, watching her intent face with a half smile.

Once they had sailed Phyllida went back to her cabin to unpack. They wouldn't get back until Wednesday morning and she would need some clothes—evening clothes especially. She decided on her long evening skirt and a pretty top to go with it, put everything else tidily away and went along to the lido.

The doctor was there, sitting at a table by the swimming pool, a drink at his elbow, deep in a Dutch paper he had bought in Funchal before they sailed. She hesitated, wondering if she should join him; they weren't exactly travelling together, only fellow passengers. She started back the way she had come, only to be halted in her tracks by his: 'Hey, where are you off to?'

She approached the table slowly as he unfolded his length and pulled out a chair for her. 'Well,' she said carefully, 'I just thought we're only fellow passengers, not travelling together, if you see what I mean. You wouldn't want me hanging round your neck like a millstone.'

'Wouldn't I? Get this clear, love, I'm a shy man, I don't know a soul on board and I intend to cling to you like a limpet.' He added: 'During waking hours, of course.'

He was teasing her, she knew that, so she laughed back at him.

'Well, I don't know anyone, either. Only you must tell me if I'm in the way.' She grinned suddenly, at ease with him once more. 'I saw the most gorgeous blonde just now—she really is lovely.'

He lifted lazy lids and she blinked under his intent look. 'I must chat her up, I'm partial to blondes. Do point her out.'

'She doesn't need pointing out,' remarked Phyllida with something of a snap, 'you'll see her easily enough for yourself.'

He didn't answer her, only asked her what she would like to drink.

They went down to tea presently and then played Bingo, getting very excited when they nearly won, and then going along to the shop to browse around, buying postcards she would never send and a huge tin of toffees for Willy, who would appreciate them far more than anything foreign and unedible.

She was almost dressed when Pieter tapped on her door before dinner. 'Come in,' she called, 'I'm trying to find an evening bag.'

He sat down on her bed, watching her while she searched through the drawers and at length found what she wanted. He took up so much room in the cabin that it seemed to shrink as she stepped carefully backwards and forwards over his big feet before sitting down beside him to change things from one bag to the other.

He watched her lazily. 'You look very nice— we'll dance later, shall we?'

She nodded, finished what she was doing and got to her feet.

'The bar, I think,' he suggested, 'but let's go this way; I've an urge to play the fruit machines.' He handed her a handful of silver. 'Split fifty-fifty whoever wins.'

Phyllida had never played before. She had wanted to on the voyage out, but she had never had enough time to herself—besides, she had been afraid that she might lose too much money. She won two pounds now and screamed with delight. 'Here's your money, and your half of the winnings. Now you have a go.'

He won nothing and presently she cried: 'Oh, do stop, you won't have any money left—do have some of mine.'

He declined. 'My luck's out—let's go and have a drink, we can play later if we want to.'

The bar was crowded, but they found seats in a corner and bent their heads over the next day's programme. 'I don't think I'll go to the keep fit class,' said the doctor seriously, 'and definitely not the fancy dress—how about deck quoits and a nice long lie in the sun doing nothing?'

Phyllida agreed happily. And that was how they spent their days, swimming in the pool before breakfast, playing some deck game or other after breakfast and then lying side by side doing nothing, not even talking. Phyllida found it singularly restful; the sea was calm, even in the Bay of Biscay, and the weather stayed fine, although as they neared their journey's end there was a decided nip in the air, which made sweaters a necessity, and when they got too chilly, Pieter pulled her to her feet and made her play table tennis. They danced each evening too; the only fly in the ointment was the blonde girl. They had a table for two in the centre of the restaurant and the girl was seated close by in the doctor's direct line of vision. She was an eyeful, Phyllida decided vexedly on their first evening, and she couldn't compete with the white crêpe dress, cut low and with a long gored skirt which twisted and twirled as the girl walked the length of the restaurant. She had piled-up hair, dressed in a careless riot of curls and crowned with a tiny cap sporting a curling feather which curved round one cheek—absurd on anyone else, but on this girl, devastating. The doctor had studied her at length and with no expression.

'I told you I wouldn't need to point her out,' said Phyllida.

He gave her one of his bland looks. 'Oh, I do see exactly what you mean, love—she's a knock-out.'

She had agreed with chilly enthusiasm.

As far as she knew, he hadn't looked at the girl again that evening, nor the next morning. It was after lunch when he told her that he was going down to the purser's office, and strolled away.

He was still gone an hour later, and with nothing to do, she remembered that she had to press a dress for the evening. She was on her way to the ironing room when she saw them standing near the purser's office, deep in conversation. The girl was leaning back against the wall, her hands on either side of her, pressed against it, a beguiling attitude calculated to show her figure off to the best possible advantage. She was looking up at the doctor with a look which Phyllida had often tried before her looking glass, without much success because she had always giggled. She sped on down to the deck below, sure that she hadn't been seen, did her pressing and hurried back. They weren't there when she reached the purser's office.

She hung up the pink crêpe—really it had been a waste of time fussing with it, the doctor wasn't going to notice, was he? not with that creature making eyes at him—and bounced out of her cabin and back to the deck, to be waylaid at once by a young man with a lot of teeth and pebble glasses who asked her eagerly if she would like to use his binoculars. There was nothing to see, but she agreed with an enthusiasm which encouraged him to offer her a drink. It was nearly tea-time and not really warm enough for a cold drink, but he looked so anxious to please that she accepted a lemonade and stood at the rail with him, drinking it while he told her all about his job— something vague in the City.

She wasn't sure when she first felt that they were being watched; after a moment or two she looked round cautiously. Behind them, lying in a chair with his feet up, was the doctor. He grinned as she turned a shoulder to him.

She finished the drink slowly, aware that it was four o'clock and everyone was going down to tea, and trying to decide whether she should stay where she was and wait for Pebble Glasses to invite her to share his table, or excuse herself, ignore the doctor, and have tea on her own.

She knew that she was being childish and silly, which made it more difficult to decide. Luckily it was decided for her; the doctor tapped her smartly on the shoulder, smiled with charm at her companion and wanted to know if she was coming to pour his tea for him. Short of saying no, she wasn't, there had been nothing she could do about it. Out of ear-shot of Pebble Glasses he had observed placidly: 'Paying me back in my own coin, Phylly?'

'I don't know what you're talking about.' She tried to sound dignified, which was quite wasted on her companion, who sat her down in a quiet corner and fell to examining the plate of cakes on the table between them. Only when he had done this to his satisfaction had he said: 'Empty as a hot air balloon.' He looked at her, smiling faintly. 'What a pity—such beauty, and nothing—just nothing between the ears.' He sighed: 'But I found it interesting from a medical point of view.'

His voice was so silky that she shot him a suspicious glance. 'I don't believe it.'

He hadn't appeared to hear her. 'Now you, love, have good looks and a good brain to go with them— you'll make someone an excellent wife one day.' He added wickedly. 'Was Pebble Glasses all you could find?'

It had been impossible to be grumpy with him after that.

Phyllida packed with great regret before dinner on their final evening; she had been to the purser's office and got herself a seat on the coach which would take any passengers who wished up to Victoria Station, but she hadn't told Pieter. And he for his part hadn't said a word. She supposed that they would say goodbye after an early breakfast and she would never know where he was going. Somewhere in England? Holland? She had no idea.

They were watching a spirited entertainment after dinner when he said in a tone which brooked no denial: 'I've arranged for a car to be at the dock. I'll drive you home.'

She had been surprised at the delight which swept through her.

'But it's miles away...'

'Three hours run at the outside.'

'Well—but don't you want to go home?'

His smile told her nothing. 'I've two or three days to spare, I should enjoy the drive.'

Which really didn't answer her question.

CHAPTER FIVE

DISEMBARKING FROM the ship at Millwall Dock was smoothly efficient and swift. Phyllida found herself and her baggage on the road outside the dock with hundreds of others, only whereas they were getting on to a fleet of coaches, taxis or relatives' cars, she had been led to a corner and told to stay there while Pieter went to look for his car. He was back inside five minutes, driving a Ford Scorpio, and long before the buses had revved up their engines he had stowed the luggage, popped her into the front seat, got behind the wheel and driven away.

It was still barely nine o'clock in the morning and the traffic in the East End was dense; it got worse as they approached the city, but the doctor didn't allow that to irritate him, he kept up a gentle flow of talk weaving in and out of the traffic unerringly so that presently Phyllida asked: 'Do you know London well? You drive as though you did.'

'I come here from time to time. I'm aiming for the M3, I think it'll be best if we cut straight through, don't you, and cross the river at Chiswick. We can stop in Richmond for coffee, and what about

Salisbury for lunch? Isn't there a place called the Haunch of Venison?'

'Yes, but I'm sure Mother would give us a late lunch, there's really no need...'

He shot her a quick smile. 'Oh, let's have a last lunch together, shall we?—Perhaps your mother will be kind enough to invite me to tea.'

It was while they were drinking their coffee in Richmond that Phyllida suddenly realised that she hadn't thought of Philip for days. She looked across at the doctor, scanning the headlines of the *Telegraph*, and thought how nice it was that they could sit together like this without making conversation because they felt that they should. Every now and then he read out some item which he thought might interest her, but he made no special effort to capture her attention; he might have been her brother. She wasn't sure whether to be annoyed about this or not. Upon due reflection she thought not, for although they hadn't known each other long they had an easy friendship, quite at ease with each other and enjoying each other's company. But that was all; he had never shown any signs of interest in her as a person. Indeed, the blonde on board had come in for more attention...

She frowned into her coffee. She wasn't a vain girl, but she was aware that she had more than her share of good looks and although she had no sophistication to speak of, someone had told her once that she was a wholesome girl. She had quite liked it at the time, now she wasn't so sure; she didn't think that Pieter would be interested in wholesomeness—he had, she considered, an experienced eye. She sighed and he put the paper down at once. 'Sorry—my shocking manners. Let's go.'

It began to rain as they started off again and by the time they got to Salisbury it was a steady downpour. But the Haunch of Venison was warm and welcoming; they ate roast beef and Yorkshire pudding and treacle sponge afterwards, and accompanied this nourishing meal with a bottle of claret. It was still raining when they got back into the car, and as they drove through the dripping countryside Phyllida felt a pang of disappointment that the first sight of her home should be marred by a grey, wet day. But her companion didn't share her view. As they went down the hill to the village and she pointed out her home on the opposite rise, he stopped the car to have a look.

'Early Georgian?' he asked.

'Partly. There's a bit at the back that's Queen Anne. It's a pity it's wet.'

'It's beautiful—rural England at her best.' He looked at her. 'Excited?'

She nodded. 'I always love coming home. I don't think I ever enjoyed living in London. I like pottering in the garden and going to the village shop and walking miles. That must sound very dull.'

She was surprised when he told her: 'I live in the country myself—not as lovely as this, but beautiful in a placid way. No hills like these.'

He started the car again, driving slowly now, and stopped again outside her home.

He was an instant success. Her mother, pottering around the window boxes along the front windows, turned at the sound of the car, crossed the narrow strip of pavement and peered through the window at them.

'Darling, how lovely, and you've brought someone with you.' She beamed at the doctor and added: 'How very nice,' because his smile held such charm.

He got out, opened Phyllida's door and when she had embraced her mother and introduced him, said in his placid way: 'I'm delighted to meet you, Mrs Cresswell. I hope it's not inconvenient...?'

Mrs Cresswell's smile widened. 'It's the nicest surprise, and how kind of you to drive Phylly home. Come in, I was just going to get the tea. There are rather a lot of us, I'm afraid.' She glanced at Phyllida. 'Willy's home again, he's been very under the weather, poor boy, and Beryl's home for a few days—so's Dick—half term,' she added vaguely, 'or whatever it is they have at these places.'

She paused to take a good look at her elder

daughter. 'Darling, you're nice and brown, but you look—well—come inside and tell me about it.'

She glanced across at the doctor standing quietly by. 'There's something, and you'll know about it too, I expect. Come into the kitchen while I get the tea; the others won't be in for a bit. Willy's gone with Father on his visits and the other two went over to Diggs' farm.'

Mrs Cresswell had the happy knack of putting people at their ease and making them feel at home. The doctor was offered a seat at the kitchen table, given a pile of scones on a dish, a plate of butter and a knife, and asked if he would split and butter them. Phyllida, sitting opposite, making sandwiches, was surprised to see how handy he was; as far as she could remember he hadn't done a hand's turn at the de Meesters' house, although of course there he hadn't really needed to.

Her mother was taking a large cake from its tin. 'Well, darling?' she looked questioningly at Phyllida. 'Or shall Doctor—no, I shall call you Pieter—talk about it?'

Phyllida started to spread the sandwiches. 'Gaby died. We were put ashore at Funchal because the ship's doctor was worried about her and thought she ought to go home or into hospital. The de Wolffs left us at an hotel and went on with the ship. I—I found her unconscious and Pieter got her into hospital and fetched the de Wolffs back, then he took me to stay with some friends of his until there was another ship.'

Her mother received this somewhat bald statement calmly. 'Very distressing—poor Gaby, and poor you, darling. We have to thank Pieter for a great deal.' She glanced at the doctor's impassive face. 'Phylly, be a dear and run down to Mrs Brewster's and get some more cream—we haven't nearly enough for these scones.'

And when the door had closed behind her daughter: 'Neither my husband nor I will be able to thank you enough, Pieter. And now the child's out of the way, will you tell me exactly what happened?'

He sat back in his hard chair, his hands in his pockets. After a moment he began to tell her in his calm way, not taking his eyes from his listener's face. When he had finished Mrs Cresswell said again: 'Thank you, Pieter—just to say that isn't enough, but I don't know what else... Will you tell my husband when he comes in? After tea while we're washing up.' She added: 'Those wretched de Wolffs, what I'd like to do to them!'

The doctor nodded without speaking and then with his eyes on the door behind her: 'I can see that you're an excellent cook, Mrs Cresswell. Can you cook, Phyllida?'

'Of course she can,' Mrs Cresswell took her cue

smartly. 'I taught her.' She took the cream from Phyllida and emptied it into a china dish just as the front door banged shut. 'Beryl and Dick,' she lifted her voice. 'We're in here.'

She had just finished introducing everyone when Doctor Cresswell came in too and it all had to be done again. 'And now we all know each other,' said Mrs Cresswell happily, 'let's have tea.'

It was a noisy meal with everyone talking at once, asking questions of Phyllida and not really listening to the answers, which was just as well, for she was quieter than usual. But they supposed her to be tired after her journey, although once or twice her father was on the point of asking her a question, but the doctor had intervened smoothly each time. It wasn't until the meal was over and Mrs Cresswell marched everyone into the kitchen to help with the washing up, bestowing a speaking glance at her husband as she did so, that Doctor Cresswell, left with his guest, observed: 'I gather there is something I should know. Am I right?' He got up. 'I think if we went to the study—Willy stayed out to tea, but he'll be back at any time—we might get interrupted here.'

His guest told him exactly what he had told Mrs Cresswell but without any glossing over of the harsher bits. Doctor Cresswell heard him out without comment.

'Poor little Gaby. I'll go and see the de Wolffs

tomorrow. I'm deeply indebted to you for looking after Phylly and doing what was best for Gaby. And these friends of yours, I should like their address if I may, so that we can express our thanks to them as well.'

He got to his feet. 'You'll stay the night, of course—longer if you can manage it.'

'I should be delighted; I still have a few days before I need to go back.'

'Then spend them here. Do you suppose that Phylly wants to talk to me about this?' Doctor Cresswell's nice open face crinkled into a smile. 'We're the greatest of friends and I don't want to force her—perhaps she'd rather wait...'

'I think she would like to tell you herself. She was very upset about it, although she did everything possible in the most difficult of circumstances.'

'She shall drive me on my morning rounds.' Doctor Cresswell led the way into the hall and across it to the large, airy sitting room. 'Are you a G. P. like myself or do you specialise? I gather from the talk at tea that you live in the country...'

In the kitchen her mother said to Phyllida: 'Of course Pieter will stay the night. Beryl, run up and make sure that the cubbyhole is just as it should be.'

Beryl giggled: 'Mother, isn't he a bit big for it? Hadn't he better have the room next door? Phylly and I can make up a bed in no time.'

Mrs Cresswell nodded to her younger daughter, as dark as Phyllida was fair, small and pretty too. 'Of course, dear, he is rather big, isn't he—he might be a bit cramped.'

Phylly finished drying the tea things. The cubbyhole was kept ready for Willy's friends from school or the younger nephews and nieces. She smiled at the idea of Pieter trying to fit his bulk into the narrow bed. 'Very cramped,' she agreed. 'I'll come now, Beryl.'

They all sat down to supper later, and Willy, who should have been in bed because he still wasn't quite fit, somehow managed to persuade his mother that he was well enough to stay up. It was a nice old-fashioned meal, with cold meat and pickles and potatoes baked in their jackets smothered in butter, and a very large rice pudding with cream and raisins for afters. Phyllida watched Pieter a little anxiously, remembering the delicious food they had had on Madeira and on the ship, but she need not have worried. The doctor consumed a vast supper with every sign of content and enjoyment.

Going upstairs to bed later, it struck her that she had exchanged barely a dozen words with him during the whole evening, although his goodnight had been as friendly as it always had been. Tomorrow, she promised herself, she would find out when he was going.

Only she didn't. True, they met at breakfast, but by the time she had helped with the washing up and made the beds, her father was calling for her to drive him on his morning round, and Pieter and Beryl were at the other end of the garden, picking the rhubarb from under its forcing bucket, ready for one of her mother's super pies.

'I've heard it all from Pieter,' her father told her as they started off down the hill, 'but I'd like to hear it again from you, Phylly.'

It was a relief to talk about it, she felt better when she had told him about it, and better still when her father said: 'You did all you could, you have no reason whatsoever for blaming yourself. Put it behind you, my dear. Have you thought what kind of job you want?'

She hadn't; somehow she hadn't been able to put her mind to thinking about her future and she said so.

'Then take a holiday,' advised her father.

They got back a little late for lunch, and found the doctor in the kitchen, sitting in one of the old Windsor chairs by the Aga, his long legs stretched out on the rag rug at his feet. Willy was there too and Dick as well as Beryl and her mother. They looked as thick as thieves.

Everyone turned to look at her as she went in, and it was Dick who said: 'Hi, Phylly—we've

hatched a simply super scheme.' He grinned round
at the doctor, who was standing, staring at nothing.
'You tell her, Pieter.'

She looked at them in turn. Their expressions reminded her forcibly of Meg, their elderly spaniel,
when she hoped for a biscuit, all except the doctor,
who looked half asleep. Phyllida sat herself down
on the edge of the table, picked up a raw carrot from
the dish and began to crunch it, and asked: 'Well?'

The doctor sat down again. He looked quite at
home in the rather shabby old kitchen, just as though
he had been a family friend for years. 'I have been
talking to your mother about the flowers in Holland
at this time of the year. Bulbs, you know, fields full
of them and a rather special park where one can go
and see them all growing in a charming setting. I
live quite near the bulb fields and I wondered if she
might like a brief holiday so that she might see them
for herself—Willy would come too, of course,' he
sounded very bland, 'a few days' holiday might set
him up ready for school again. Only there is one
snag; Willy and I would like to go fishing and we
don't feel that we can leave your mother alone while
we fish, and as I'm told that if she accompanied us
she would only remove the hooks from the fishes'
mouths and throw them back into the water, I feel
that it would be hardly conducive to our enjoyment.'
He contrived to sound sad. 'She would be lonely.'

He gave Phyllida a long look. 'We wondered if you would consider joining the party?'

It was a neat trap and she wondered which of them had thought it up. 'I must look for a job.'

The doctor's voice was all silk. 'You did tell me that you might take a holiday first.'

She bit into the carrot. 'Father…' she began.

He answered smoothly. 'We did—er—discuss it vaguely yesterday evening, after you had gone to bed.'

The trap had closed and she was amazed to find that she felt nothing but pleasure at its closure. All the same, she wasn't a girl to give in tamely. 'How will Father manage?' She looked at her mother.

'Beryl will be home for at least another two weeks—she doesn't get her exam results until then and the job she's after depends on those—she might just as well be here, and she'll love to look after him, and Dick can come down for the weekends.' Her mother smiled so happily that Phyllida, peering at her from behind her fringe, knew that she couldn't disappoint her; she didn't have many holidays.

She said quietly, 'I'd love to come. When?'

There was a kind of concerted rush towards her, while her family, all talking at once, told her. When they paused for breath, Pieter said from his chair: 'In three days' time, if that suits everyone?'

Phyllida was sure that by everyone, he meant her;

the rest of them would have already agreed happily to anything he might have suggested—even her father, who had just walked in, exclaiming: 'Well, is it all arranged? It's most kind of you, Pieter. My wife is a great gardener, nothing will give her more pleasure, but I do hope you know what you're taking on—three of them—you're sure you can house them all?'

The doctor answered him gravely. 'Oh, yes, I think that can be done. I hope you'll allow them to stay as long as possible—ten days? Two weeks?'

Willy looked anxious. 'If we're going fishing, two weeks would be super—I mean you have to work as well, I suppose?'

'I suppose I do,' he was gravely assured.

So Phyllida spent a good deal of the next two days unpacking and packing again, helping her mother to do the same, and going through Willy's wardrobe. Which left Beryl free to entertain the doctor, for Dick had gone again. She made a success of it too, judging by the way she made him laugh.

They left after breakfast to catch an afternoon Hovercraft from Dover, seen off by Doctor Cresswell, Meg the spaniel, an assortment of cats and Beryl, looking fetching in a large apron. She had flung her arms round Pieter's neck as she wished him goodbye and given him a hug and begged him to come back soon, and he had said something softly to make her laugh and kissed her soundly. Phyllida wondered why she was going and not Beryl. It should have been the other way round.

Their journey was a pleasant one, with a stop for an early lunch and a great deal of talk, mostly on Willy's part, concerning the joys of fishing, until they reached the Hovercraft, when he switched to engineering. Neither topic interested the two ladies of the party; they listened with one ear to make sure that Willy wasn't being rude or cheeky and carried on a desultory chat about clothes, the chances of Beryl remembering that her father couldn't stand lamb cutlets at any price, and what sort of presents they would buy to take back with them. But once on board, the conversation became general while they drank coffee and ate sandwiches and listened to their host explaining the rest of the journey to them.

It was well into the afternoon by now and it seemed that they still had a fair distance to go. They would land at Calais, travel up the French coast into Belgium and from these cross over into Holland at Sluis, then take the ferry to Vlissingen and from there drive all the way to Leiden on the motorway. He lived, explained the doctor, in a village bordering one of the lakes a mile or so from that city.

'Handy for your work, I expect,' chatted Mrs Cresswell. 'Do you have beds in a hospital there?'

'In Leiden, yes, also in den Haag.'

'Ah, yes,' said Mrs Cresswell knowledgeably, 'Leiden's a medical school, isn't it?'

So now we know, thought Phyllida, a thought peevishly, all this while and never a hint as to exactly where he lived—to her, at any rate.

They were actually disembarking at Calais when she wondered about the car. They had left the one he had hired in England and she hadn't given it another thought. She glanced round her and the doctor answered the question she hadn't asked. 'It's waiting for us, it should be over here.'

It was—a Bentley, not a new model, but a much cherished fifteen-year-old motor-car, sleek and gleaming and powerful. There was a man standing by it, a corpulent, middle-aged man, with a bald head and a round, cheerful face. The doctor spoke to him, shook his hand, and waved to a porter to load the luggage. The man had gone before that was finished and the doctor installed his guests without saying who he was.

'Such a nice car,' observed Mrs Cresswell, 'and what a lot of room!'

'Yes, I think so too—I've had her for a long time now and she suits me perfectly. She has a good turn of speed, too.'

Which proved to be the case. They went so fast through France, Belgium and then into Holland that

Phyllida was hard put to it to know just where they were. Only as they crossed on the ferry to Vlissingen was there time to pore over a map while they drank coffee in the bar on board, and then she didn't take it all in, there was so much to see from the deck.

The spring evening was turning to dusk under a wide cloudy sky as they took the road northwards; Bergen-op-Zoom, Rosendaal, Dordrecht, by-passing them all, so that there was nothing to see of the actual towns. But there were plenty of villages, with their great churches and neat clusters of houses, and in between, wide water meadows striped with canals. Phyllida, sitting in the back with her mother, looked about her with interest. It was so very different from Madeira, from England even, but she liked it—it was calm, placid country and only as they skirted the bigger towns was she aware of factory chimneys and bustling industrial areas. It was nice when the doctor turned off the motorway on to a secondary road which took them across country to join another motorway just south of Leiden. He left this too after a few miles to turn down a country lane, brick built and with a canal on either side of it. They were back in the country again and presently she could see water; a wide lake stretching away into the dusk. The road ran beside it for some distance until they reached a village. 'Leimuiden,' said the doctor. 'The next one is Kudelstaart; I live just half way between them.'

There wasn't a village when he slowed the car presently, just a group of houses and cottages and a very small church, and then a high brick wall pierced by wrought iron gates, wide open.

The sanded drive was straight and quite long and the house at the end of it was so unlike anything that Phyllida had expected that she gave a gasp of surprise. It was a large square building, painted white, with single-storey wings on either side, connected by short covered passages. Its orderly rows of windows and all the ground floor ones were lighted, illuminating the great front door with its elaborate decoration of plasterwork picked out with gilt.

'How very grand,' observed her mother, who had a habit, sometimes embarrassing, of saying what came into her head. 'I'm quite overwhelmed—it's a good thing it's almost dark,' she added obscurely. But her host understood, for he assured her:

'It's not in the least terrifying, even in broad daylight, and I'm told it's wickedly inconvenient to clean.'

Willy hadn't said anything, but now, as they stopped on the sweep before the door, he observed: 'I say, what a super place for a holiday—I'm glad I came!'

The doctor laughed and got out to open doors and usher his guests out of the car, and by then the house door had been opened too and a welcoming light streamed out to meet them from the hall beyond.

There was a tall thin woman standing just inside, looking so exactly as a housekeeper looked that there was no mistaking her; dressed severely in a dark grey dress, neat greying hair pulled back into a bun, a sombre face; but when she smiled she wasn't sombre at all, and she was delighted to see the doctor, who flung an arm round her as he introduced her.

'This is Lympke, my friend and housekeeper. She doesn't speak English but I'm sure you'll manage to understand each other. Her husband, Aap, who brought the car to meet us, will be here presently and he speaks it very well.'

He swept them all inside, through the wide hall and a pair of arched doors into a high-ceilinged room of vast proportions. It had wide windows at one end and at the other there were a few shallow steps which led to another, much smaller room, lined with books. The furniture was exactly right for its surroundings; glass-fronted cabinets filled with silver and porcelain, splendid wall tables carrying vases of flowers, a lacquered cabinet—and nicely arranged between these antique treasures were sofas, wing-backed armchairs and a variety of tables. The walls were white, the panels picked out with gilt and hung with paintings, mostly portraits, lighted by crystal sconces.

The doctor waved them to chairs amidst this splendour. 'Tea?' he enquired of Mrs Cresswell, unerringly guessing her one strong wish, and at her pleased nod, said something to Lympke who had followed them in. She went away and returned almost at once with a tea tray which she set on a small table by Mrs Cresswell's chair and while the two ladies drank their fill, the doctor gave Willy a glass of lemonade, pouring a whisky for himself.

'You have a very nice home, Pieter,' observed Mrs Cresswell, passing Phyllida her tea. 'I had no idea—you told Ronald that you were a GP and I hardly expected...'

Phyllida stirred uneasily and hoped that the doctor wouldn't take umbrage. He didn't, only saying mildly: 'Well, I do have a surgery here in the house, you know, and quite a few local patients, but I must confess that most of my work is done in den Haag and Leiden, and sometimes abroad.'

'What do you specialise in?'

He smiled very faintly. 'Among other things, hearts.' He was looking at Phyllida, who knew what he was and kept her eyes fixed on a family group on the wall opposite her.

'Now isn't that nice?' asked Mrs Cresswell of the

room at large. Neither of her children answered her because she had a habit of voicing her thoughts aloud and didn't expect anyone to reply anyway, but the doctor chose to do so.

'Well, I enjoy it; it's work I'm deeply interested in and it's a challenge.'

'Yes, of course.' Mrs Cresswell was well away. 'And you, you poor man, without a wife and children, you must be lonely.'

Phyllida gave her mother a look which that lady ignored, and the doctor's smile widened. 'I haven't been until now; just recently I have found that work isn't quite enough, though.'

He was still looking at Phyllida, who felt rather like a rabbit with the snake's eye upon it. She would have to look at him, she couldn't help herself; she withdrew her gaze from the family group, whom she now knew very well indeed, and met his eyes.

'You agree, Phyllida?' he asked blandly, then smiled so brilliantly that she found herself saying fervently:

'Oh, yes, I do! Work's very nice, but it—it…' She had no idea what she was going to say, but sat there with her pretty mouth open, praying for some witty, clever remark to come into her empty head.

It didn't, and his smile became the merest twitch of the lip.

'Would you like to go to your rooms?' He was

the perfect host again. 'We'll dine in an hour's time if that's not too late for you, but do come down when you would like. I shall be around, but if I'm not, do make yourselves at home.'

Lympke led the way upstairs, up a handsomely carved staircase at the back of the hall, leading to a wide corridor above. Phyllida and her mother had adjoining rooms at the side of the house, while Willy, to his delight, was given a small room at the back of the house, well away from them. He could just see the gleam of water from his window even though it was almost dark now and came running back to tell them so.

'That's where we'll fish,' he told them importantly. 'I'm going down to talk to Pieter; someone's unpacked for me, so there's nothing for me to do.'

'You'll wash your face and hands, comb your hair and take a clean handkerchief,' decreed his mother, and when he had gone: 'How beautiful these rooms are, Phylly, and such heavenly bathrooms. Are you going to change your dress?'

'No, I don't think so, just do my face and hair and change my shoes.' Phyllida wandered over to the window and stared out into the evening, although she could see almost nothing by now. She said thoughtfully, 'It's a pity he's rich—I didn't know...' She sighed. 'And not just rich, he's—well...'

'Yes, dear, but he'd be that whether he had money or not, wouldn't he? And remember that your father's family is an old and honoured one.'

'Mother,' Phyllida's voice was rather high, 'I don't know what you're talking about.'

Her mother's reply was placid. 'No, dear, I often don't know either. Shall I back-comb my hair a bit in front? My head's as flat as a snake's after wearing a hat all day.'

They went downstairs presently and found the drawing room empty, but almost at once the fat man they had seen at Calais appeared at the door. 'Aap, madam, miss—the doctor's houseman. If you should want anything I will arrange it.'

They thanked him and Phyllida said: 'What good English you speak, Aap. Have you been in England?'

'Certainly, miss. At times I travel with the doctor, you understand. We also stay there from time to time—the doctor has many friends.' He smiled at them. 'The doctor and your brother have gone to look at the lake. It is now dark but Master Willy wished to see it for himself. It is not large, but there is a canal which leads to the *meer* beyond.'

He crossed to the windows and drew the heavy tapestry curtains, tended the log fire in the wide hearth, begged them to make themselves comfortable, and withdrew.

Mrs Cresswell sank into a deeply cushioned chair and sighed with pleasure. 'The last time I was in a house like this one was when I was ten years old—your Great-Aunt Dora at Weatherby Hall, dear. Such a pity she had to sell it.'

Phyllida had perched herself on a velvet-covered stool near the fire. 'Well, I like our house,' she declared a shade defiantly, 'it's beautiful and old and it's home.'

'Well, of course,' observed the doctor from the doorway, 'but home can be anywhere, can't it? A cottage or a semi-detached or an isolated farm—it's how one feels about it, isn't it?'

She had turned round to face him. 'I'm sorry,' she said quickly, 'I didn't mean to be rude; this is a lovely house and it's home for you, just as my home is for me.'

He smiled slowly. 'I hope that when I marry, my wife will love this house as much as I do. You must explore it one day.'

He had crossed the room to where a tray of drinks stood on a carved and gilded table. 'What will you ladies have to drink?'

He brought them their drinks and went back to get a Coke for Willy and a Jenever for himself. 'I don't need to go to the hospital until after lunch tomorrow,' he told them, 'and surgery should be over by half past nine. Willy and I thought we might do a little fishing, if you don't mind being left to your own devices. Lympke will be delighted to take you over the house and there's plenty to see in the gardens, please go wherever you wish.' He sat down in a great chair opposite Phyllida. 'I thought that we might go to the Keukenhof one day soon, it should be at its best now. It's not far from here and we could leave here after breakfast—I'm afraid I'll have to be back around tea time, though, for any evening patients I may have at my rooms in Leiden.'

They dined presently in a room a good deal smaller than the drawing room but still pretty large. It was furnished in mahogany, gleaming with endless polishing and age, and the table silver and glass almost out shone it. They sat at a round table, large enough to take a dozen people with ease, although they occupied only a part of it, sitting near enough to talk comfortably.

They ate splendidly; caviar for starters, salmon poached in white wine, chicken cooked in cream with a Madeira sauce. Willy hardly spoke, but ate with the deep pleasure of a growing boy who was hungry; it was left to the other three to carry on an undemanding conversation mostly about gardens and growing vegetables and the difficulties of protecting everything from frost. Phyllida, who was a willing but amateur gardener, marvelled at Pieter, who seemed evenly matched against her mother's expert knowledge. Surely it was enough, she thought a little crossly, that he was apparently a very successful man in his own profession, had a house like a cosy museum and the good looks to turn any girl's head; he didn't have to be a knowledgeable gardener as well.

Even the appearance of a honey and hazelnut bavarois, which tasted even better than it looked, did little to lift her spirits, although she did her best to look intelligent about greenfly and black spot while she ate it. She would excuse herself when they had had their coffee, she decided, on the grounds that she wanted to wash her hair before she went to bed, but in this she was frustrated. Pieter invited her mother to telephone her father, suggested that Willy might like to have an early night so that he would feel fit for a morning's fishing, and invited her to sit down and keep him company.

'For we don't seem to have exchanged more than a dozen words,' he observed pleasantly.

'Well, I'm not mad about gardening,' she said grumpily, and then remembering her manners: 'I'm sorry, I don't know what's the matter with me—I don't mean to be so beastly rude to you. I think...' she paused and looked at him with puzzled blue eyes, like a small girl with a problem. 'I think it's because all this is a surprise. I thought you'd have a house in a village, a bit like ours—and it's not.'

'You don't like it?' he asked in a gentle voice.

'Oh, I do—it's out of this world.' She added shyly: 'I feel as though I'm trespassing.'

'Oh, never that.' She wondered why he looked amused and it was on the tip of her tongue to ask why when her mother came back into the room, and soon after they went to bed, leaving him standing at the foot of his magnificent staircase. Her mother had already gained the corridor and was out of sight when he called Phyllida back.

'I forgot this,' he told her, and kissed her, hard.

CHAPTER SIX

PHYLLIDA WENT DOWN to breakfast after a somewhat wakeful night. Naturally enough, being a pretty girl and a perfectly normal one, she had received her share—rather more, perhaps—of kisses. She had enjoyed them too, but somehow Pieter had been different from the others. She had told herself several times during the night that it was because he was older and more experienced, but she knew that wasn't the answer. She had given up wondering about it then and gone to sleep.

The doctor wasn't at breakfast, nor was Willy, who had risen early, breakfasted with his host and then taken himself off to spy out the land around the lake. Phyllida assured her mother that she had passed a dreamless night, ate her breakfast under the fatherly eye of Aap and declared that she was going to explore the gardens; for some reason she felt shy about meeting Pieter and the gardens seemed an unlikely place for him to be in at that hour of the day; he had said something about morning surgery...

She had half expected her mother to accompany her, but Mrs Cresswell had found a splendid book

137

on gardening in the library. 'I'll come out later,' she decided, 'when the sun's really warm.'

So Phyllida fetched a cardigan and found her way outside. Now that it was morning, and a bright one even if chilly, and she could see everything clearly, she had to admit that the house was charming; solid and unpretentious despite its size, fitting exactly into the surrounding formal lawns and flower beds and trees beyond. Moreover, everywhere she looked there was a blaze of colour; tulips and hyacinths and scilla and the last of the daffodils. She walked round the side of the house, peering into the wide windows of the wing she was passing. She supposed that it must be a ballroom, for it took up the whole area and its floor was waxed wood. The ceiling was painted, although she couldn't see it very clearly, and from its centre hung a chandelier, its crystals looped and twined into an elaborate pattern.

There were windows on the other side too and she walked on, rounded the wing and found herself facing a formal garden with a square pond bordered by masses of flowers and sheltered by a beech hedge. There was an alley leading from its far end and she went to look at it. It was arched by more beech, trained to form a tunnel, and that in its turn opened into a charming circle of grass, well screened by shrubs and with stone seats here and there. Right in the middle there was a wheelbarrow, loaded with earth and with a spade flung on top of it. It looked as though someone had just that minute left it there, and she looked round to see if there was anyone about, but she saw no one, neither in the alley from whence she had just come, nor on the neat brick path which led away from the grassy plot on its other side. She sat down on one of the seats and blew on her fingers. It might be the end of April, but it was still chilly unless the sun shone.

'It'll be pleasantly warm once the morning mist has gone,' observed the doctor from somewhere behind her.

She jumped. 'I thought you were taking your morning surgery.'

'My dear girl, we keep early hours here; surgery's from eight until nine o'clock and there are seldom more than a dozen patients, often less.'

He sat down beside her and she said doubtfully: 'But I thought you had a practice.'

'Well, I have, but I see most of my patients at my rooms in Leiden—this surgery is just for the villages close by.'

'Oh, I see—and you have beds in a hospital too?'

'In several hospitals.'

She gave him a searching look. 'I think you must be someone quite important.' And when he didn't answer: 'A consultant or a specialist—or do you teach?'

His eyes were smiling. 'Some of all three.' He picked up her hand and held it between his. 'You're cold. We'll walk down to the lake and see if Willy has fallen in, if he hasn't we'll bring him back for coffee before we get down to this business of fishing.'

As they started along the path, he added: 'I wondered if you would all like to come into den Haag this afternoon, you could look at the shops while I'm at the hospital. I shall only be a couple of hours and I'll show you where to go.'

She was very conscious of his hand holding hers; it was firm and warm and impersonal and she wondered again why he had kissed her on the previous evening. 'That sounds nice,' she said, her voice cool because she didn't want to seem too friendly.

They had come to the end of the path and were crossing rough ground at the end of which she could see the lake, and Willy, sitting on a log by it. Pieter had slowed his pace. 'My mother and father are coming to dinner this evening,' he said casually.

'Your mother and father?' Surprise made her repeat his words like an idiot. 'Oh, I didn't know— that is, do they live here?'

'They have a house on the coast near Scheveningen. My father is a doctor but retired now. I have two brothers and two sisters—my sisters are married, both living in Friesland, my youngest brother is in Utrecht, finishing medical school, and Paul, who is a year or so younger than I, is married and lives in Limburg—he's a barrister.'

He hadn't volunteered so much information in such a short time since they had met. Phyllida digested it slowly. Presently she asked: 'Then why do you live here, all alone in this great house?'

'When my father retired he and my mother went to live on the coast because the house—a charming one—is close to the golf course and he enjoys a game. It was always understood that they would go there eventually and it's like a second home to us all, as we spent our holidays there when we were children.' He sat down beside her. 'And as I'm the eldest son, I took over here. I don't regret it.'

'It's very large for one person.'

His eyes were almost shut. 'Yes, but it's surprising how a clutch of children fills even the largest of houses.'

'But you haven't any children.'

'Something which can be remedied.' He changed the conversation so abruptly that she was startled. 'I think you'll like the shops in den Haag—will Willy be bored?' He turned to look at her. 'I could take him with me; I'll get someone to take him round one or two of the more interesting wards until I'm ready—he's really keen on becoming a doctor, isn't he?'

She agreed, secretly put out. She would have been interested too, and she might have found out something of his life while she was there; his working life, but it seemed that he didn't want her to know. Well, if he wanted to be secretive, let him. 'I said I'd go and find Mother,' she told him.

They had a splendid afternoon wandering round the shops, buying inexpensive trifles to take home, drinking tea in a smart café and then walking back to the spot where Pieter was to pick them up. The journey home was occupied almost exclusively by Willy's observations about what he had seen, the doctor's mild replies and Phyllida's slightly cool ones, which she regretted when he asked her in the friendliest possible manner if she would go with him on the following day in order to choose a birthday present for his younger sister.

'I've no ideas at all,' he assured her, 'and if you would be so kind as to advise me...'

She agreed at once, and the rest of the ride was taken up with a lighthearted discussion between Willy and his host concerning the chances of them landing a good sized pike when next they fished the lake.

Phyllida was a little apprehensive about meeting Pieter's parents; while she dressed she tried to imagine what they would be like and failed; the doctor was an enormous man, probably his parents would be of a similar size, on the other hand, very small women quite often had large sons. She put together a mental picture of his mother, small and dark and terribly smart. She combed her fringe smooth, put on a thin wool dress in a flattering wine shade, and went downstairs.

Her mother and Willy were already there, she could hear their voices through the half open drawing room door—other voices too. Aap, appearing suddenly, opened the door wide, and she went in.

The master of the house was standing against one of the display cabinets, one hand in a pocket, the other holding a glass, his long legs crossed, his shoulders wedged against the dark woodwork. He was talking to a very tall, very large lady, with elegantly dressed white hair, handsome features and what Phyllida described to herself as a presence. Across the room, talking to her mother and brother, was an elderly man, as large and powerfully built as the doctor and just as good-looking. The three of them made a formidable trio, and she wondered briefly if his brothers and sisters were the same size; no wonder they lived in such an enormous house.

The doctor came to meet her, his compelling hand urging her forward to where his mother was standing. That lady surprised her very much by saying mildly, before any introductions had been made: 'My dear, I'm sure Pieter didn't warn you about us—being so large, you know—when the whole family are together I've known people turn pale at the sight of us.' She laughed, a deep rich chuckle which transformed her austere appearance.

Why, thought Phyllida, taking the offered hand, she's just like Mother, only larger.

Pieter had been standing between them, now he said placidly: 'I don't think Phyllida is easily frightened, Mama.' He smiled a little. 'What will you drink, Phylly?'

He fetched her a sherry and took her to meet his father. It was like talking to Pieter, they were so very alike; the same hooded blue eyes, the same firm mouth and patrician nose, only his hair, still thick, was quite white.

She sat beside him on one of the vast sofas, while the others gathered together on the other side of the hearth, and he talked of nothing much in particular, putting her at her ease, and presently when Aap came to announce dinner, they went, still laughing and talking, to take their places round the beautifully appointed table. Phyllida, sitting beside the elder of the van Sittardts with Willy on her other side and Pieter's mother next to him, noticed with some amusement that her brother was getting on splendidly with his neighbour, which left her mother and Pieter, talking quietly together.

The evening was an unqualified success; the mag-

nificent dinner helped, of course, and the glass or
two of claret she drank with it, but even they
wouldn't have been of much help without the easy
charm of her host and his parents. She found herself
quite anxious to meet the rest of the family.

Only one thing marred the evening for her. Sitting
round the fire, drinking their coffee, Mevrouw van
Sittardt took advantage of a pause in the talk to ask:
'And have you seen Marena yet, Phyllida? I feel
sure that you must have, as she spends a great deal
of her time here. She and Pieter are very old
friends—lifelong, one might say, and he has grown
accustomed to be at her beck and call at all times.'

The lady smiled as she spoke, but Phyllida had
the strong impression that she would have preferred
to have ground her teeth. She said that no, she hadn't
met the girl in question yet, and glanced at the doctor, sitting with her mother. He looked as blandly
impassive as usual, but she had no doubt that he had
heard every single word, for his mother had a clear
and ringing voice. She wished very much to ask
about this Marena; it seemed strange that if she were
such a close friend—perhaps more than a friend—
Pieter should never have mentioned her. It wasn't
her business anyway, she told herself sternly, and
plunged into an account of their shopping expedition
that afternoon; probably she would never see the
girl.

She was wrong. They met the very next day, after Phyllida and the doctor had returned from a highly successful search for the birthday present. The afternoon had been fun although short, for he had had a number of private patients to see at his rooms in Leiden, and hadn't been able to pick her up until the middle of the afternoon. Nevertheless, the next hour or so had been delightful, especially when she discovered that there was no reasonable limit to the amount he might be called upon to spend. They chose a pendant finally, a dainty thing of gold with a border of rose diamonds, and then had tea before going back home, where Willy had immediately waylaid them and badgered them into a rather wild game with Butch, the nondescript old dog who was Pieter's devoted slave. Phyllida had cast off her jacket the better to run faster and was tearing across the lawn towards the house with Butch in hot pursuit when she saw a girl watching them from the terrace. She was small and slight, with large dark eyes and a pouting mouth, expertly made up; she made Phyllida feel tall and fat and untidy. Untidy she certainly was, for the sun had come out and was shining warmly so that her face was flushed and her hair blew wildly around her head, sadly in need of a comb.

The girl smiled charmingly as she crossed the lawn to join them, but there was malice with the charm and Phyllida sensed that the girl had already decided that there was no competition for her to fear. Her eyes spoke volumes for Phyllida to read—this guileless outdoor type with great blue eyes and a gentle mouth and a fringe like a little girl wasn't Pieter's type. The smile widened as she reached Pieter, tucked an exquisitely cared for hand under his arm and said in accented English: 'Darling Pieter, have you missed me very much? And how good it is that you have friends to amuse you while I am not here.' She gave his arm a little pat and gave a trill of laughter. 'But now I am.'

He smiled down at her. 'Nice to see you, Marena—how's the painting?'

She made a charming face. 'Not good, not good at all. I need your opinion, otherwise I shall destroy all that I have done. Will you come and look at them?'

'Yes, of course. Still at the studio, are you?' He turned to Phyllida. 'Phylly, meet Marena. She paints, and she's good at it, too.' His amused gaze swept over her untidy person and she flushed. She said politely:

'How interesting. I've never met an artist, it must be wonderful to be able to paint.'

'Anyone can learn,' Marena assured her sweetly, and dismissed her. 'Pieter, can I speak to you for one minute? It is important and private.'

Phyllida was at the door before she had finished speaking; she could take a hint as well as the next one and Marena clearly wanted her out of the way. 'I must tidy myself,' she muttered. 'I expect I'll see you again before we leave—so nice meeting you.' She wrenched open the door and ducked through it, casting a totally meaningless smile over her shoulder as she went.

Willy had melted away as only boys can, and Aap, crossing the hall as she stood a little uncertainly, offered the information that he and his mother had gone down to the lake to see if they could find the swan's nest there. There was still plenty of time before dinner; she flew upstairs and without bothering to do more than run a comb through her hair, flung on a cardigan, and using the back stairs, went out of the house. Somehow she couldn't bear to join the doctor and Marena again—indeed, she thought it unlikely that they would want her to. A good walk would do her good and if she returned with only enough time to change for the evening, the chance of meeting the girl again would be slight, although she might stay for dinner.

'And why should I care?' asked Phyllida loudly of the trees around her. 'Well, I do, anyway.' And indeed, to be quite honest, she had begun to think that Pieter had fallen a little in love with her, and she, moreover, had fallen a little in love with him.

She stopped her brisk walking, struck by a sudden blinding thought. She wasn't a little in love with him; she was head over heels; no one and nothing else mattered in the world. Never to see him again would be a sorrow she wouldn't be able to bear, and it was a sorrow she wouldn't be able to share with anyone, least of all Pieter. At all costs she would have to hide her feelings. They would be going back home in ten days or so and she would have to be very careful. She walked on faster than ever, trying to escape the awful thought that she had allowed him to see that she liked him very much. Well, she could soon put that right. Cool friendliness and steering clear of anything personal when they were talking—that would leave him free to dote on his precious Marena. She ground her splendid teeth at the thought.

She turned for home presently, for she had been out too long already, and reached the garden door just as Pieter came out of it. He was looking preoccupied although he smiled when he saw her.

'Hullo there,' he said easily, and there was a glint of amusement in his eyes as he took in her flyaway appearance. 'You've been out and I thought you were still doing things to your hair. I've just left a message with Aap—I'm afraid I'll have to go out this evening and I do apologise to you all. I doubt if I'll be back until late.'

He held the door for her to go through. 'By the way, Marena wants us all to go over for drinks before you go back—may I tell her that you would like to?'

He was going to spend the evening with the horrid creature. Phyllida said in a cool little voice: 'Why, of course—we shall be delighted. How very kind.' She gave him a bright smile and hurried past him.

Mrs Cresswell made no comment when Phyllida told her that their host would be out for the evening, but Willy asked anxiously: 'Did he say when he'd be back? We're going fishing at four o'clock tomorrow morning.'

'Don't worry, dear,' soothed his mother, 'I'm sure Pieter wouldn't forget anything as important as that.'

But hours later, listening to the stable clock chiming twice, Phyllida wondered if he had, and she was sure of it when half an hour later she heard the Bentley whisper past her windows.

She slept after that, a miserable exhausted sleep which left her heavy-eyed and snappy, and when Berta the housemaid brought her her morning tea, she had no desire to get up. All the same, she went down to breakfast presently and found her mother and brother already there. Her mother wished her good morning and ignored her pale cross face, but Willy was less perceptive. 'I say, Phylly, you do look cross. We had a smashing time...'

'You went fishing? But Pieter…' She stopped herself in time. 'I didn't think Pieter would get up so early.'

'He wanted to,' said Willy simply.

'One can always find time to do what one wants,' observed her mother comfortably. 'Phylly, pass me another of those delicious rolls, will you? It's such a splendid morning, I think I'll take that gardening catalogue Pieter lent me and go and sit in that dear little summer house. What are you two going to do?'

'I'm going to the next village,' said Willy importantly, 'the one you can see across the fields from the side of the house. I have to deliver a note for Pieter; one of his patients has to go into hospital.' He buttered himself some toast with a lavish hand. 'We're all going to the Keukenhof the day after tomorrow, he told me so this morning.' He sighed with content. 'I caught two bream this morning and Pieter got four.' He wolfed down the toast. 'Phylly, are you coming with me?'

She agreed readily. Her own company was something she wished to avoid at all costs, and presently they set off into the bright morning, pleased with each other's company despite the dozen or so years between them, Phyllida rather silent and Willy talking non-stop.

'It was super of Pieter to come this morning,' he

told her. 'He's been up most of the night, you know—that case at the hospital in Leiden.'

'What case?' asked Phyllida with instant interest. 'And how do you know?'

Her brother gave her a kindly, impatient look. 'He told me, of course—this boy had a relapse, so he was called in for a consultation. He's very important, you know.'

'Is he?' she asked humbly. 'I didn't know—he never said.'

'Well, of course not,' said Willy with scorn. 'I mean, a man doesn't go around boasting. But he's frightfully brainy—I expect he'd have told you if you'd asked—I did.' His chest swelled with pride. 'He knows I'm going to be a doctor when I'm a man, he says I'm a natural because Father's a doctor anyway and it's in the blood, like it is in his—he says you can't help yourself if it is and that I'll make a jolly good one. He talks to me just as though I'm grown up.'

Pieter loomed large in Willy's life, that was obvious, but then he loomed even larger in hers. She sighed. 'Oh, does he? What exactly does he specialise in, dear?'

They were almost at the village and had slowed their pace.

'Hearts—you heard him say so, didn't you? And

leukaemia, didn't you know that either? And you're always talking to him...'

'Am I?' asked Phyllida sadly. But not, it seemed, about anything that really mattered. She wondered what Pieter really thought of her behind that calm, handsome face. Probably nothing much.

Willy discharged his errand and they walked back, having a one-sided conversation about fishing, with him in full spate about lines and hooks and flies and she saying yes and no and really, while she allowed her mind to dwell upon Pieter, so that she followed her brother in through the garden door rather dreamily, to bump almost at once into the master of the house, lying back in a large cane chair in the garden room, his feet on another chair, fast asleep.

They stood and looked at him for a moment and Phyllida saw how weary he was, with lines etched on his face which she hadn't noticed before, a faint frown between his brows. Willy wandered away, but she went on staring and then gave a squeak of surprise when the doctor asked softly: 'Why do you look like that, Phylly?'

'Like what?'

'Motherly and sad.' He unfolded himself and stood up, smiling.

'Oh—oh, I don't know. I'm sorry if we woke you up.'

'I'm not. Let's get Aap to bring some coffee to the summer house. I saw that your mother was there.'

So they all had their coffee together and he didn't say a word about where he had been or why, indeed, he presented the perfect picture of a man of leisure, only presently he went to sleep again and Mrs Cresswell and Willy crept away, leaving Phyllida sitting there with him. She wasn't sure why she wanted to stay, perhaps because it was wonderful just to be there; presently he would go off again and she wouldn't know where, or perhaps Marena would come frisking along to make him laugh. Two large slow tears trickled down her cheeks; she was only half aware of them and didn't bother to do anything about them and there was no one to see.

'Why are you crying?' asked the doctor softly.

She was so vexed with herself that she could hardly speak. She might have guessed that he wasn't asleep, but he had looked so tired. She didn't answer, only looked away from him, wiping the tears away with a finger.

'No job?' he persisted. 'An uncertain future? Not happy here, perhaps?'

'Oh, I am, I am. It's lovely—I thought when I first came that it was all so grand, but now I know just what you meant about it being a home, because it is.' She went on in a muddled way: 'Cats on the chairs and that nice old dog and the way you fling your jacket down on that magnificent table in the hall, and your mother and father...'

The doctor's eyes gleamed beneath their lids, but all he said was: 'Then you must be in love.'

She went red, and then, unable to stop herself: 'Yes, I am—I've only just found out, though I think that I knew days ago. It's funny...'

It was fortunate that she was interrupted, for she had flung caution to the winds and had actually started to tell him that she was in love with him. She froze with horror and for once was glad to see Marena crossing the lawn and smiling with the air of someone who was sure of a welcome. She flung her arms round the doctor's neck and kissed him with what Phyllida considered to be a sickening display of sentiment and then smiled at her. Her voice was gracious.

'Hullo—you look much nicer today, but I do not like your fringe. Fringes are for little girls, are they not? And you are no longer that.'

Phyllida tried to think of a suitable answer to this snide remark, but her head was still full of the things she had so nearly said; she felt sick just remembering them. The doctor answered for her: 'You're wrong, Marena, Phylly isn't grown up at all, not nearly as grown up as you are. And I like the fringe.'

'I am but nineteen,' declared Marena prettily, and perched on the arm of his chair.

'In years, in worldly knowledge, double that.'

She pouted and dropped a kiss on to his head. 'I do not know why I like you so very much, Pieter.'

'Nor I. Without wishing to be inhospitable, I should warn you that I am about to leave for my rooms. What do you want this time?' He sounded amused.

'Darling, I need some money and the bank say no more until my allowance is paid. If I could have five hundred gulden—just till then—I will pay back...'

He put a hand into a pocket and fished out a roll of notes. 'Here you are. A new dress, I suppose.'

Marena took the notes and stuffed them into her handbag, flashing a triumphant look at Phyllida. 'Of course—such a charming one. I shall wear it for you when you come.'

'I look forward to it.' He submitted to another embrace and with a careless wave of the hand for Phyllida, Marena skipped off. A moment later Phyllida heard a car start up and roar away.

'She's the world's worst driver,' murmured the doctor, and closed his eyes again.

Phyllida sat and looked at him, suspicious that he was only foxing again, but presently he snored, very faintly, but still a snore. She gave him ten minutes and then ventured: 'I say, you said you had to leave…'

He opened one eye. 'Did I really say that? Then I made a mistake—I have nothing to do until this evening, when I have to give a lecture at a hospital in Utrecht. You can come with me if you like.'

She sat up very straight. 'May I really—I'd like to.'

'Good. And now shall we finish that very interesting conversation we were having when we were interrupted? You were saying?'

'Nothing.' She couldn't get it out fast enough. 'It wasn't anything, really it wasn't.'

'No?' His tone implied disbelief. 'Ah, well, later on, perhaps.' He smiled at her and her heart bounced so that she caught her breath.

'I thought we might go to the Keukenhof the day after tomorrow,' he told her. 'It should be looking at its best; your mother is anxious to inspect the flowers.'

Phyllida was glad of the change in the conversation. 'Yes, she's a great gardener…' She babbled on for a few minutes and then stopped a bit abruptly; even in her own ears she sounded foolish.

They dined early by reason of the lecture and then drove the forty miles to Utrecht. The evening was fine and the country as they approached the city looked pretty and peaceful. 'But not as pretty as where you live,' declared Phyllida.

'Well, I do agree with you there, but I daresay I'm prejudiced.' He swept the car through the main streets, worked his way through some very narrow lanes and entered the hospital courtyard.

She was given a seat near the back of the lecture hall and made to feel at home by the young doctor who had been asked to look after her. She hadn't given much thought to the lecture. That it was delivered in Dutch really didn't matter; it was bliss just to sit there and stare at Pieter, elegant and assured and presumably amusing, for every now and again there would be a burst of laughter around her. He had a lovely voice, she thought, deep and a bit gravelly and unhurried. She sighed gustily and the young doctor gave her an anxious look which she dispelled with a beaming smile.

On the way home, later, Pieter observed idly: 'It can't have been much fun for you—did you go to sleep? I must have been out of my mind to have asked you in the first place.'

'Oh, but I loved it, and I didn't go to sleep—I listened to every word,' and when he gave a great shout of laughter: 'Well, you know what I mean.'

'I like to think that I do.'

A remark which gave her plenty to think about until they got back.

She saw little of the doctor during the following day, though, surprisingly, Phyllida thought. His mother called in the afternoon and had tea with them, going round the gardens with her mother, enjoying a long talk about flower growing.

'I like her,' declared Mrs Cresswell when Mevrouw van Sittardt had been driven away in an old-fashioned, beautifully kept motor-car. 'She's a bit overpowering, but she's a woman after my own heart.' She added by way of explanation: 'She doesn't cut her roses back either.'

The doctor arrived home in the late afternoon, waved aside offers of tea and disclosed the fact that they were all going to Marena's studio for drinks before dinner. Phyllida instantly went into a flurry of hair brushing and fresh make-up, deploring the fact that the weather had turned quite warm and she really had nothing to wear. It would have to be the thin wool, which meant that after the first drink and with the central heating, she would be as red as a beet in no time at all.

Marena's flat was in the centre of den Haag, high up in a modern block, all black marble entrance and chromium fittings, and her studio was very similar— a vast room with paintings stacked along one wall and an easel under one enormous window. It was furnished in a modern style and its walls hung with Impressionist paintings, a fitting background for

Marena who was wearing an outrageous outfit; a tunic slashed to the waist and tight velvet pants. Phyllida eyed her with real envy, wishing she dared to dress like that; it might capture Pieter's attention.

And it did, but not in the way she had expected. He took a long look and said slowly: 'If that's what you borrowed five hundred gulden for, my dear, it's been wasted.'

Phyllida saw the flash of anger in the girl's eyes although she laughed at him. 'It's not for you, Pieter—I've a new boy-friend.' She flashed a look at Phyllida, who looked back at her woodenly.

They drank a concoction in long glasses which Phyllida didn't like but didn't dare to say so, and yet it must have shown on her face, for while Marena was showing Mrs Cresswell her paintings, Pieter crossed the room and took the glass from her and gave her his empty one. He must think her an awful baby, she mused sadly.

They stayed a couple of hours, which gave Phyllida ample time in which to watch Marena at work on Pieter, who was treating her as one might treat a pretty child; goodnaturedly answering her preposterous remarks, praising her paintings, telling her that she was getting prettier each time he saw her. Phyllida, feeling a frump in the woollen dress, registered a firm resolve to go out the very next day and buy some new clothes. It wasn't until they were on the way home that she remembered that they were going to spend the whole of the next day at the Keukenhof.

CHAPTER SEVEN

THE KEUKENHOF WAS beautiful under a cloudless sky, although a chilly wind set the flowers nodding and swaying. They had left the house shortly after breakfast and driven the few miles there in no time at all, so that when they reached the park there were very few people about. They strolled round while the doctor and Mrs Cresswell exchanged Latin names and methods of propagation in an assured manner which left Phyllida and Willy quite at sea. But whatever they were called, the tulips and hyacinths and daffodils were a colourful sight, arranged in glowing patches of colour so that whichever way one turned there was something to delight the eye.

'Mind you,' remarked Mrs Cresswell, 'your own gardens are magnificent and must take a good deal of planning.'

The doctor laughed. 'I must plead guilty to leaving most of the work to Bauke, who has been with the family for so long I can't remember what he looked like as a young man. He's a wizard with flowers—I only study the catalogues and say what I like.'

'Do you ever garden yourself?' asked Phyllida, remembering the wheelbarrow and the spade.

'Oh, yes—the odd hour or so when I have the time; it's good exercise. And you, Phyllida?'

They had paused to allow Willy to investigate a stretch of ornamental water. 'Me? Well, I dig potatoes and pull carrots and cut the flowers if I'm home. What's that building over there?'

'A restaurant and café. If you won't get too chilly we might have coffee on the terrace before we go along to the glasshouses.'

Which they did, sitting near the water in the sunshine, and then wandering on again towards the great greenhouses. The gardens were lovely, but the display in the houses took even Mrs Cresswell's breath. She hurried from one spread of colour to the next, exclaiming over each of them, and: 'Oh, how I wish I could take them all home with me!' she sighed.

'Hardly possible, I'm afraid, but you must allow me to offer you a small memento of your visit— we'll pick out the bulbs you particularly admire and I'll order them—you'll get them in the autumn.'

'Oh, I couldn't!' and then at his gentle smile: 'Well, just one or two, perhaps.' She went happily all the way round again, trying to make up her mind which she would choose. 'Those Kaufmanniana hybrids for the rock garden, perhaps—or should I have that alium Moly, such a lovely colour.' Her eyes wandered to the display of parrot tulips. 'That blue and mauve one—if I might have one or two?'

'Do you care for the Mendel? I have them at home, if you remember—such a good colour in spring, I find.' The doctor was quietly leading her on. 'The clover pink goes so splendidly with the iris danfordiae—an unusual colour scheme, but you must admit that the pink and yellow made a splendid show.'

'Oh, yes—I did admire them in your garden. It's hard to choose—perhaps if I might have a few iris and one or two of the parrot tulips? And thank you very much.'

Mrs Cresswell looked quite flushed with pleasure.

'I'll go across and order them from the office there. Do go on looking around; I shall find you presently.'

Mrs Cresswell pottered off happily enough, pointing out what she would have if only she could afford them. Which gave Phyllida an idea. She would buy some bulbs for her mother too; if she went back to the little rustic hut where they took the orders she would be able to see which ones the doctor had ordered and get something to go with them. She muttered her plan to Willy and slipped away.

The doctor was still there and she was surprised to see the look of guilt on his face when he saw her.

She didn't pause to consider this, however, but plunged at once into her idea. 'And if you'll tell me what you've ordered I'll get something else,' she finished.

Something in his face made her transfer her gaze to the clerk holding the order book. A whole page of it was filled and she turned a questioning look upon Pieter, who gave her a calm stare which told her nothing. 'It seems a pity,' he remarked blandly, 'that your mother shouldn't have something of everything she admired; I should like to think of your garden at home filled with flowers—she likes them so much.'

'The whole lot?' she gaped at him.

'Well, not quite all.' He smiled faintly. 'Now you're here, will you help me to decide which of the tulips to have in my own garden? That pink lily flowering one is charming—you were admiring it...'

'I think it's super, but why ask my advice? I mean, you'll be the one to see them, not me. But if I were choosing for my garden, yes, I'd have them. Where will you plant them?'

'In the beds on either side of the front door, under the windows. I'd better have two hundred.'

She gulped. 'That seems an awful lot,' she ventured.

'There's an awful lot of garden,' he pointed out,

and took her arm. 'Let's find your mother and Willy—and not a word, mind.'

They had lunch presently in the restaurant and then a last stroll before driving back. At the house once more, Phyllida, wondering what to do with the rest of her afternoon was over the moon when the doctor suggested casually that she might like to go with him to his rooms.

'I'll be there a couple of hours,' he said. 'You can look round if you're interested and then while away the time at the shops until I'm ready.' He glanced at her mother, happily immersed in a pile of catalogues, and Willy, already on his way across the lawns with the dog. 'I don't think you'll be missed.'

His rooms were in a narrow street of elegant houses, with barely room to park a car before their doors. He stopped the Bentley half way down and got out to open her door. 'If you walk to the end and turn to the right, you'll be in the main shopping centre. This is Finklestraat and I'm at number ten. If you get lost, just ask the way back.'

He was on the ground floor; a richly comfortable waiting room, an office where his secretary sat and a consulting room beyond and beside it a small treatment room. There was a nurse there, a formidable middle-aged woman who greeted the doctor austerely and immediately took him to task for something or other. He listened meekly to her lecture, said something to make her laugh, and led the way into his consulting room. It was of a pleasant size and furnished in soothing shades of grey and soft browns, with comfortable chairs and a large desk. She looked round her slowly. 'You're a very successful man, aren't you, Pieter?'

His lips twitched. 'I work hard, Phylly.'

'Oh, I didn't mean to be rude—I only meant...'

He caught her hand. 'I know that. I wanted you to see where I work for a good deal of my day.' He bent and kissed her lightly. 'Now run along and enjoy yourself. You can have two hours.'

She found herself in the street, her head a muddle of thoughts and dreams. Perhaps he was falling in love with her, on the other hand he could be being just friendly, wanting her to enjoy her holiday. There was no point in brooding about it. She walked briskly to the end of the street and made for the nearest shops.

Egged on by the thought of Marena, she was tempted to enter a boutique presently, and once inside she cast caution to the winds and bought rather more than she had intended; a silk jersey tunic in a dusky pink, a pleated skirt in pale green with a matching jacket and a real silk blouse to go with them, and lastly a cotton jersey shirtwaister in pale amber; she hadn't meant to buy that, but the saleslady had pointed out, quite rightly, that it would be a most useful garment for the rest of the year.

Much lighter in the purse, and in the heart too, Phyllida found her way back to Finklestraat and poked her head round the waiting-room door. The room was empty and she had a sudden pang that everyone had gone home and left her behind; instantly dismissed as absurd, for the Bentley was still standing at the kerb.

She sat down with her packages around her and waited quietly until the nurse came out, followed by the secretary. They both smiled at her and the secretary said: 'The doctor is coming,' as they went out.

Pieter joined her a few minutes later, opened his sleepy eyes wide at the sight of her parcels, observed that she had put her time to good use, swept them up and ushered her out to the car. He seemed disinclined for conversation, so after one or two tentative remarks Phyllida gave up and sat silent until they stopped at his house. There was another car parked on the sweep and as he leaned over to open her door, he observed a little impatiently: 'And now what does Marena want, I wonder? Not another dress so soon?'

Phyllida received her parcels, thanked him for the outing and went ahead of him into the house; if Marena was there she didn't want to see her. Even so, she was illogically put out when the doctor made no attempt to delay her. He watched her make for the stairs, Aap behind with her purchases, before turning away and going into the drawing room.

Once in her room, Phyllida lost no time in trying on everything she had bought. The jersey tunic was certainly stunning. She decided to wear it that evening; it might possibly detract Pieter's interest from Marena. She had heard the car start up and leave, so she would have a clear field.

She went downstairs presently, feeling a little excited, aware that she looked her very best. It was a great pity that Pieter wasn't there. Aap tendered his excuses and begged that they would dine without their host, and offered no further information at all.

Phyllida received her mother's admiration of her new dress with a pleasant calm which concealed rage, carried on a spirited conversation with Willy about the size of the fish he might one day catch, and dinner over, declared that she had a headache and retired to her room, where she threw the new dress into a corner and cried herself to sleep.

The doctor, returning home presently to spend the rest of the evening with his guests, evinced surprise when Mrs Cresswell told him that Phyllida had gone to bed with a headache, but he said nothing beyond murmuring some civility or other, poured himself a whisky and sat down in his chair. Mrs Cresswell, studying him while he exchanged a bantering conversation with Willy, concluded that he looked thoughtful, but not in a worried way; more as though he was mightily pleased about something.

Phyllida went down to her breakfast the next morning with some caution. She didn't want to meet Pieter, not yet, not until her puffy eyelids were normal again. He should be gone, either to his surgery or to one or other of the hospitals he visited. All the same, she approached the breakfast room circumspectly and was about to peer round its half open door when his study door was flung open behind her. His cheerful: 'Ha!' uttered in a booming voice, sent her spinning round to face him.

She managed: 'Oh, good morning—I thought you'd gone?'

He leaned against the door frame, watching her. 'So who were you expecting to jump out on you?'

She had regained her breath and her composure. 'No one. I expect you're just off to the surgery.'

'Indeed I am. But I shall be back. It is unfortunate that I can't take Willy sailing as I'd arranged, but there are a couple of urgent cases I must see. Besides, I fancy this weather isn't going to last and the *meer* can be quite nasty if the wind rises.' He wandered towards her. 'Your headache is quite better?'

'Headache?' She remembered then. 'Oh, yes— yes, thank you—it wasn't a bad one.'

He said with faint mockery: 'I thought it wasn't.

A pity that I should have returned home so soon after you had gone to your room.' And when she didn't answer: 'Well, I won't keep you from your breakfast. We shall meet at lunch, I hope.'

Her mother was too wise to ask after the headache. She launched into a rambling chat about a letter she had had from Doctor Cresswell, and Phyllida, listening with half an ear, wondered why Willy looked so glum. She wasn't kept in the dark for long.

'We should have gone sailing,' declared her brother. 'I was looking forward to it no end, and now Pieter says he can't—not today.' He made a hideous face. 'And you'll see, it'll be raining tomorrow and if it's fine he'll have more patients to see...'

'Well, he is a doctor,' Phyllida pointed out reasonably, 'and you've had a lot of fun—fishing and so on.'

Willy buttered toast and spread it with a slice of cheese. 'Yes, I know—it's been super, but there's only another week.'

'Well, let's do something else,' suggested Phyllida. 'Any ideas?'

'I think I'll borrow the bike in the garage and go for a spin.' The look he gave her was so angelic that she instantly suspected that he was up to something, but surely a bike ride was harmless enough.

'OK, I've got some letters to write. How about you, Mother?'

Mrs Cresswell looked vague. 'There was something—Oh, yes, I remember now, Bauke is going to take me round the glasshouses and the kitchen garden. We shan't understand a word each other's saying, but I don't see that it will matter.'

So they all dispersed to their various morning activities and it wasn't until a few minutes before lunch time that Phyllida, wandering into the garden room, wondered where everyone was. Her mother arrived just as she was thinking it and burst at once into an account of the delightful morning she had spent with Bauke. 'A taciturn man,' she observed, 'but a most knowledgeable one. We're going to spend another hour or two together before we go back. Where's Willy, dear?'

Phyllida had one ear cocked for the doctor's firm tread. 'I don't know, Mother—still cycling, I expect.'

'Not at all likely,' remarked his parent sapiently. 'He'll be near home; it's too near lunch time.' She sat down and sighed contentedly. 'See if you can find him, Phylly, he's sure to be grubby.'

There was no sign of him in the gardens near the house. Phyllida went further afield, exploring the shrubbery paths, peering in the summer house and garden sheds, even the garages behind the house.

The bike was still there and she frowned at the sight of it and went on down to the lake, its waters ruffled by a chilly little wind coming in gusts, shivering as she went, for the watery blue sky was clouding over rapidly. It took her a minute or two to register the fact that the yacht which had been moored to the jetty by the boathouse wasn't there, and another minute to find Willy's school blazer flung down carelessly beside the path.

He'd taken the yacht. That accounted for the innocence of the look he had given her at breakfast; he had meant to all along. Phyllida ran along the narrow path bordering the lake and then followed it beside the canal which led to the wide *meer* beyond, and presently reached its edge.

Quite close inshore was the yacht, just ahead of her, bowling merrily along—much too fast, she thought—before the blustery wind, and she could see Willy quite clearly in it. As she looked he caught sight of her and shouted something and waved, then turned away so sharply that she thought the boat would heel over. Surely Willy would have enough sense to hold the rudder steady? Apparently he hadn't, for the yacht was careering towards the centre of the *meer* and he was getting further away with every second.

She looked around her, seeking inspiration, trying not to feel frightened. There was a promontory half a mile further along the bank, standing well out into the water. If she could reach it before Willy she might be able to guide him towards it and beach the yacht. It was to be hoped that they could tie the yacht up; she worried for a minute about Pieter's reaction if they damaged it and then dismissed the thought; it was more important to get Willy out of his fix. She began to run, urged on by the rising wind and the first few drops of rain.

She reached the spit of land ahead of Willy, now heading away from it once more, and she hurried to its very edge, filled her lungs and bawled at him to steer towards her. 'Turn the rudder slowly,' she counselled at the top of her lungs, and almost before she had finished the yacht swung violently towards her, its sail almost touching the choppy water. 'Gently!' she called, and waited anxiously as the boat came towards her, much too fast. It wasn't like Willy to behave in such a way; he could do most things well and he had a solid common sense which had got him out of any number of awkward situations. Now he was waving at her and calling, but before she could catch what he was shouting, the yacht careered off again, only to turn in a few moments and come towards her once more, this time within hailing distance.

'What's up?'

'The rudder's broken.' He didn't sound too upset.

'I've got an oar and I'm trying to steer with it, but it's not much good.'

Phyllida had kicked off her shoes and tossed her cardigan onto the grass bank. 'Keep her steady if you can, I'll come out to you.'

She wasn't a strong swimmer and the water was very cold. And worse, Willy wasn't having much success in keeping the yacht on the same course. It was pure luck that the boat swerved towards her, coming so close that she was able to cling to its side, to be hauled aboard with a good deal of difficulty.

She subsided on to the deck, wringing wet, smelling of weed. 'Willy, I'll wring your neck!' she said forcefully, and then: 'What do we do first?'

Willy ignored her threat. 'If we both hang on to the oar—or perhaps we could tie it with something?'

'What?' She looked around her; the yacht was immaculate with everything in its place, but she didn't dare touch the ropes arranged so neatly in case something came adrift and they were worse off than ever.

'We'll hold it,' she decided, 'and try and steer to the bank somehow.' She looked up at the sky, shivering. The wind, freshening fast, had brought the rain with it.

She said suddenly: 'Willy, is there a horn?'

He gaped at her. 'A horn? Yes, of course—it's used when you go through a lock. Why?'

'Can you remember the Morse Code?'

'Yes, of course I can.'

'Well, do it on the horn. Is it three short, three long, three short, or the other way round?'

Her brother gave her a withering look. 'Girls!' he uttered with scorn. 'Can you manage the oar for a bit?'

Her teeth were chattering now; she was already so wet that the rain made no difference, except to make her feel worse. 'I'll have to, won't I? Willy, why did you do it? Have you any idea what Pieter is going to say when he discovers that you've taken his boat?'

'He's going to be angry—I daresay he'll ask us to go home.'

'Oh, you wretched boy! Go and blow that horn, for heaven's sake!'

Mrs Cresswell waited for ten minutes or so and then wandered to the window and looked out. There was no sign of either of her children; it was fortunate that Pieter was late for lunch; they might get back before he did. But after another ten minutes she became uneasy. She drank the sherry Aap had poured for her in an absent-minded fashion and wondered why they were so long—perhaps they could all come in together.

But presently the doctor came in alone, took one look at her face and asked: 'What's worrying you, Mrs Cresswell?'

'Well, I'm not exactly worried. I daresay I'm just being a fussy old woman...' She explained simply, adding: 'Willy did say that he was going to borrow the bike in the garden shed.'

The doctor went to look out of the window. 'We can check that easily enough,' he assured her, and pulled the bell rope by the fireplace, and when Aap came spoke briefly to him.

Aap went away and returned within a few minutes. The bicycle was still in the shed, he reported impassively.

'So he's fishing.'

Aap shook his head. All the rods were in their rightful places; he had looked on his way back from the garages. The doctor frowned, took another look at the rain and wind outside, then opened the french window and glanced around. It was while he was doing this that he became aware of the insistent blast of the horn.

He listened for a moment. 'Someone is sending out what I presume to be an SOS,' then: 'My God, it's the *Mireille*—that young devil's got her out on the *meer*!' He swung round. 'Aap, get me a jacket.

Mrs Cresswell, don't worry, I'll be back with Willy and Phyllida very shortly.'

He took the anorak Aap was holding out to him, gave a satisfied grunt when he saw that Aap was putting on a similar garment, and made for the garden. Mrs Cresswell watched the pair of them walking briskly across the lawn, to disappear presently behind the shrubs at the far end.

The moment they were out of sight they broke into a run, the doctor covering the ground with his long legs at a great rate, and Aap, for all his stoutness, close on his heels. They followed the path Phyllida had taken and reached the edge of the *meer* in time to see the yacht veering away towards the opposite shore.

'What the hell...?' began Pieter furiously. 'Aap, I believe they've lost the rudder, and why don't they get the sail down?' His face was coldly ferocious. 'We'll get the speedboat out and get alongside her. Stay here—I'll pick you up.'

He went back, running fast, to the boathouse by the lake, and within a very short time came tearing through the canal, to pick up Aap and then roar out into the choppy water.

Phyllida, wrestling with the oar, watched his rapid approach with mixed feelings—relief, because she didn't want either Willy or herself to drown, and she could see no alternative at the moment, the way they were careering around and the weather getting nastier at every moment—and apprehension as to Pieter's reaction to seeing his lovely yacht exposed to some of the worst handling he might ever witness. Willy, hanging on to the oar beside her, gave a gusty sigh.

'It's like one of the gods coming to wreak vengeance! I'm scared. Are you, Phylly?'

'Not in the least,' she screamed at him above the wind, and felt her insides turn to ice with fright. Pieter, she decided, was going to be far worse than the storm.

It looked as though she were right as the speedboat drew near. The doctor was standing, his face like a thundercloud, tearing off his anorak and then stooping to pick up a rope. If he threw it, she thought miserably, she would never catch it, she was rotten at catching things—Willy would have to do it; presumably they were to be towed in. The yacht, caught in a gust of wind, made a sweeping turn and started off merrily in the opposite direction so that she lost sight of the speedboat. But only for a moment; it roared into view once more, almost alongside, and she gave a gasping shriek as Pieter, the rope in his hand, jumped into the water. He was a powerful swimmer; before the yacht could turn again he had pulled himself on board and was tying the rope, turning to shout to Aap, still in the speed-boat, taking no notice at all of her or Willy.

Aap shortened the distance between them and when he was alongside Pieter said: 'Over you go, Willy, into the boat with Aap, and look sharp!'

There was no question of disobeying him; he might be sopping wet, his hair plastered on his head, water dripping off him in great-pools, but that made no difference to his air of command. Willy did ex-actly as he had been told without so much as a word, landing awkwardly beside Aap, who grinned at him and nodded directions to sit down. Phyllida, ex-pecting to go next, clutched the oar to her as though it were an old familiar friend and had it taken from her, none too gently.

'I would expect Willy to play those schoolboy pranks,' said the doctor in a voice which did nothing to reassure her, 'but you, Phyllida, what the hell pos-sessed you?'

He had dumped her down on the deck and was reefing the sail with swift expertise, and she didn't bother to answer. Let him think what he liked, she thought furiously; she was cold and still frightened and wet and smelly and nothing mattered any more.

Aap was sidling away from the yacht, going ahead of her and turning slowly in the direction of the canal, and presently Phyllida felt the yacht turn too, obedient to the pull of the tow rope. Pieter was hanging over the rudder, examining the break which had caused all the trouble. He turned his head to say: 'Well, you haven't answered my question. Why did you let Willy get on board in the first place?'

She pushed her soaking fringe out of her eyes. 'I didn't,' she raged at him, 'he was already in the middle of the *meer*. I had to swim out to help him.'

She choked at his amused smile. 'Swam, did you? Brave girl!' He turned away to do something to the tow rope and she said angrily to his enormous back: 'I certainly wouldn't have got on to your rotten old boat for any other reason.' Her voice shook. 'I thought Willy would drown!'

The yacht was dancing along through the rough water, the speedboat ahead, and they were almost at the canal. Pieter finished what he was doing and squatted down on the deck beside her. 'Are you very angry?' she asked in a small voice.

He flung a heavy wet arm round her shoulders. 'When I was ten—eleven, I did exactly the same thing, only the rudder didn't break. I got quite a long way before my father caught up with me. I was punished, of course, but the next day he took me out and taught me how to sail a boat.' His rage had gone, the smile he turned on her was very gentle. 'I think we'd better teach Willy how to sail too before he sinks everything in sight.'

'I'm sorry—we'll pay for the damage...' She had

forgotten her rage. 'And I didn't mean it—about it being a rotten old boat.'

'I didn't think you did. Can you sail?'

'No.'

'Then I shall have to teach you too.'

'There won't be time.'

He had got to his feet, as they were entering the canal. 'All the time in the world, love.'

They were at the boathouse and he was shortening the tow rope, calling to Aap. 'And don't do that again, Phylly.'

She was on her feet too, relieved to see the jetty and dry land but reluctant to leave him. 'Do what?'

'Terrify me to my very bones.' He said softly: 'You could have drowned.'

He lifted her on to the jetty, fetched a blanket from the boathouse and wrapped her in it. 'Whose idea was it to send an SOS on the horn?' he wanted to know in an ordinary voice.

'Phylly's,' said Willy, 'and I did it.'

'Next time, boy, get it right. OSO isn't quite the same thing, only I happened to recognise the *Mereille's* horn. Off to the house with you, tell your mother you're safe and get dry and into other clothes—you can have fifteen minutes. After lunch you and I have to talk.'

Willy went red but met the doctor's eye bravely enough. 'Yes, you'll want to punish me. I'm sorry

I did it.' He darted off, and the doctor spoke to Aap, busy with the boats, and took Phyllida's arm. 'And a hot bath and dry clothes for you, too.' He was walking her along so rapidly that she had to skip to keep up with him.

Steadying her chattering teeth, she asked: 'Am I to be talked to too?'

'There's nothing I should enjoy more,' he assured her, 'but we'll keep that until a more suitable time.' A remark she didn't take seriously.

They lunched at last, the doctor making light of the whole episode so that Mrs Cresswell shouldn't be upset. And afterwards he and Willy went along to the study, leaving Phyllida sitting uneasily with her mother in the drawing room.

'It was most considerate of Pieter to treat the whole thing as a joke,' remarked Mrs Cresswell. 'I hope he's giving Willy the talking-to of his life. Is he angry with you, too, dear?'

Phyllida glanced at her mother. She had thought they had done rather well at lunch, glossing over the whole adventure, but for all her vague ways, her parent was astute. 'I don't think so,' she said slowly.

'I should be very surprised if he were,' observed her mother. 'That girl—what's her name? is coming to tea—I heard Pieter on the telephone while you were upstairs.'

'But Mother, you can't understand Dutch.'

She was treated to a limpid stare. 'No, dear, but I happened to be sitting near him and he's far too well-mannered to speak Dutch when he knows I don't know a word.'

'Mother,' began Phyllida, 'you could have walked away.'

'So I could—I never thought of it. She's coming at four o'clock. Why not go and wash your hair properly, darling? You did it in a great hurry before lunch, I expect. It looks so soft and silky when it's just been done.'

'Mother!' said Phyllida again, then laughed. 'All right, I'll go now.'

She was glad presently that she had taken such pains with her hair and her face and that she had kept on the jersey shirtwaister. Its soft amber gave her a nice glow and contrasted favourably with Marena's flamboyant striped dress. Not that the girl didn't look quite wonderful—how could she help it with looks like hers?

Marena had driven herself over, greeted Pieter effusively, turned her charm on to Mrs Cresswell and smiled at Phyllida, dismissing her as not worth bothering about, just as she ignored Willy. A rather quiet Willy. After tea, when the other three had gone into the garden Phyllida asked him: 'Was he very cross, Willy? Did he suggest that we went back sooner, or anything like that?'

He shook his head. 'No—he gave me a good lecture.' Her brother swallowed. 'He's great, Phylly, and I like him a lot, but he can make you feel an inch high…when he'd finished he said he'd take me on the lake tomorrow if the weather was right and show me how to handle a boat.' He sighed loudly. 'I wish he was my brother.'

'You don't need any more brothers,' declared Phyllida crossly, and added severely: 'And don't you dare do anything else silly!'

The others came back then, Marena with her arm through Pieter's, looking like a sweet little kitten who'd found the cream jug.

They sat about talking for a little while longer and Phyllida did her best not to look at Pieter and Marena. The girl was at her most tiresome, talking about people only the two of them knew, leaning forward to touch his arm, smiling into his face. It was really more than Phyllida could bear. If only something would happen, she mused, something to change Pieter's manner towards her. He had always been friendly and kind and teased her a little, but she had been wrong in thinking that he was even a little in love with her. That had been wishful thinking on her part. Trying not to see Marena's lovely little hand patting Pieter's sleeve while she talked to him, Phyllida guessed that the next few days before they went home weren't going to be either easy or happy ones for her. She pinned a smile on her face now, and listened to Marena being witty about her holiday in Switzerland. To add to everything else, it seemed that she was expert on skis and even better on ice skates, and the horrid girl, drawing Phyllida into the talk, asked her the kind of questions that showed her up as a perfect fool on skates and an ignoramus when it came to skiing.

In the end, sick of the girl's barbed witticisms, Phyllida said a little too loudly: 'I'm no good at anything like that, but at least I can drive a car.' Which was a palpable hit because Marena, when she had arrived that afternoon, had knocked over a stone urn by the sweep, gone into reverse by accident, hit a tree, dented her bumper and then left all her lights on. Everyone had laughed it off at the time, but Phyllida, her gentle nature aroused, didn't see why she should get away with it.

Marena glared at her when she got up to go and ignored her as she said her goodbyes and went to the door with the doctor. When they were out of earshot Mrs Cresswell whispered, 'You were very rude, darling, but she deserved every word!'

Phyllida felt better about it then, but the feeling didn't last long, for when Pieter came back it seemed to her that his manner towards her was a little distant. Not that she cared about that in the very least, she told herself.

CHAPTER EIGHT

IT WAS disappointing that Phyllida didn't see Pieter all the next day until the evening. She had been shopping with her mother in the morning, lunching out and shopping again afterwards; they hadn't bought much, small presents for family and friends, but they had spent a good deal of time gazing into the enticing windows. By the time Aap had picked them up at the agreed rendezvous it was late afternoon, but there was no sign of their host as they sank into comfortable chairs in the small sitting room behind the drawing room and drank their tea, soothed by the peace and quiet of the old house.

'Bliss!' observed Mrs Cresswell on a contented sigh. 'I could hear a pin drop.' She took a sip of tea. 'When is Willy coming back?'

'Well, Pieter said he'd be staying to tea at the *dominee's* house.'

Mrs Cresswell ate a biscuit and followed her train of thought.

'Five more days. What a wonderful holiday we're having—I shall never forget it.'

'Nor shall I,' agreed Phyllida; she was going to remember it for the rest of her life, although perhaps

187

not for the same reasons as her mother. 'I wonder where Pieter is—he's usually home just about now.'

Her mother darted her a look over her tea-cup. 'Well, dear, he's a busy man. Besides, he must have any number of friends—after all, we don't know a great deal about his life, do we?' She took another biscuit. 'I shall get fat, but these are so delicious. A pity we aren't likely to meet again once this holiday is over. I expect we shall exchange Christmas cards and I daresay Willy will write to him.' She sighed. 'The world is full of nice people one never gets to know.'

Phyllida, surveying a future without Pieter, felt like weeping. 'The minute I get back,' she told her mother with entirely false enthusiasm, 'I shall start looking for a job. I'll try for something in Bristol, it's not far from home and it'll make a nice change.'

'Yes, dear. Have you heard from Philip since you left?'

'Philip?' Phyllida looked blank. 'Oh, Philip—no, but I didn't expect to.'

Willy came in then, full of his day and all he had done and what he intended to do the next day. He was looking very well; the holiday had done him good at any rate, thought Phyllida; it had done her mother good too—she wasn't sure about herself.

She was pouring second cups when she heard the front door close, a murmur of voices in the hall and then Pieter's firm tread. Her colour was a little high as he sat down beside her mother, although she replied to his enquiries as to her day with composure.

It was her mother who brought up the subject of their return home. 'Ought we to book our places?' she asked, 'and will you tell us which is the best way to go, Pieter?'

He took a large bite of fruit cake. 'With me, of course—in the same way as we came, in the car.'

'Oh, but we couldn't—to take you away from your work...'

He got up and handed his cup to Phyllida, and when she had refilled it, sat down beside her. 'Well, you know, Mrs Cresswell, I am able to arrange my work to suit myself to a large extent, and it so happens that I've been asked by a colleague to see a patient in London within the next week or so. I can combine business with pleasure.'

Mrs Cresswell beamed at him. 'Won't that be nice—and of course you'll stay at least one night with us—longer if you can manage it.'

He glanced sideways at Phyllida's charming profile. 'That depends on circumstances, but I hope that I shall be able to accept your invitation.'

He uttered this formal speech with such blandness that Phyllida looked at him, to be met with a sleepy gaze which told her nothing at all. She occupied herself with the teapot and left him and her mother to make conversation.

But her mother got up presently, with a murmured observation that she was to visit the rockery with Bauke before it got too late, and since Willy was bidden to accompany her, Phyllida was left with the doctor. She sat for a minute or two, thinking up plausible excuses for going away too, and had just settled on the old and tried one of having to wash her hair, when her companion spoke.

'No, Phylly, your hair doesn't need washing, nor do you wish to write letters or take them to the post. Just relax, love, I shan't eat you.'

He lounged back beside her, his eyes half closed, contemplating his well-shod feet. He looked placid and easygoing, and if truth be told, sleepy, and yet Phyllida was aware that underneath all that he was as sharp as a needle, ready to fire awkward questions at her and make remarks she couldn't understand.

'Any plans?' he asked casually.

She hesitated. 'Vague ones—well, not so vague, really. It's time I got back into hospital again.'

'London?'

Her unguarded tongue was too ready with an answer. 'No, Bristol, I thought,' and then, furious with herself for having told him that: 'Probably not—I haven't decided.'

He had moved closer, one arm along the back of

the sofa, behind her. 'That's good; I rather wanted to talk about your future, Phylly. We haven't seen as much of each other as I should have wished, all the same...' He paused and she held her breath, her heart thumping nineteen to the dozen while common sense told her that she was being a fool. In a minute she would know...

Aap propelled his cheerful rotundity through the door with a lightness of foot which made the doctor mutter something forceful under his breath.

'A gentleman to see Miss Cresswell,' announced Aap, ignoring the mutter.

Phyllida, brought down from the improbable clouds where she had been perched, said quickly: 'But I don't know any gentlemen,' and Pieter laughed. 'Ask him to come in, Aap,' he said in such a casual voice that she wondered if she had imagined the urgency in his voice not two minutes earlier.

Aap went away, to reappear almost at once, ushering in Philip Mount.

Phyllida caught her breath and jumped to her feet. 'Philip—why ever are you here? How did you find out where I was? What's the matter?'

Philip wasn't a man to be bustled into making hurried answers; he didn't say anything for a moment, only stood in the doorway, looking first at her and then at the doctor, standing beside her. At length he said: 'Hullo.'

The doctor stepped smoothly into the awkward silence. 'A friend of Phyllida's?' he wanted to know pleasantly. 'How delightful.' He crossed the room and shook Philip's hand. 'Pieter van Sittardt. I've heard of you, of course.'

His visitor shook hands cautiously. 'Oh, have you?'

'You'll want to have a talk—I'll get someone to bring in some coffee—do make yourself at home, and I hope you'll stay to dinner.'

He waved Philip to a chair, smiled benignly at him, beamed at Phyllida, standing there as though she were stuffed, and went away so quickly that no one else had a chance to say a word. Phyllida gnashed her teeth; there had been no need for Pieter to be quite so hospitable; he had almost flung Philip at her—perhaps he felt that providence, in the shape of Philip Mount, had saved him in the nick of time from saying something to her which he might have regretted. She sat down rather abruptly and Philip asked sharply:

'Who's he?'

'You heard—our host.' She had found her voice at last. 'Why on earth are you here?'

He took no notice of her question. 'He said he'd heard of me—from you?'

'Well, I suppose so.' She felt as though she had been blindfolded, turned round three times and abandoned. She asked again: 'Why are you here, Philip?'

'To see you, of course.'

'But why?'

He answered with a smugness which made her seethe. 'I knew you wouldn't forget me—and you haven't, have you? talking about me to what's-his-name.'

'Doctor van Sittardt. And I haven't been talking about you. I may have mentioned you by name, that's all.'

She broke off as Aap came in with the coffee tray, walking slowly so that he could get a good look at the unexpected guest. Phyllida poured coffee for them both, asked Philip if he wanted a biscuit in a snappy voice and waited. Philip had always been deliberate, now he was maddeningly so.

'I had a few days off,' he told her. 'I telephoned your home and your sister told me where you were. I've come to take you back with me.'

'Whatever for? I don't want to go. You're mad, Philip!' She had got to her feet. 'I'm not staying to listen to any more of your nonsense!'

He put his coffee cup down and got up too. 'It's not nonsense, Phyllida; just because you've been living it up for the last few weeks, you've lost all your good sense. I suppose you think you're in love with this fellow—well, stop your daydreaming and be your sensible self again. Come back with me and we'll start again.'

'I don't want to start again!' Her voice rose several octaves. 'Can't you understand? I don't want...' He had crossed the room and caught her clumsily in his arms.

'Don't be a silly girl,' he begged her. 'Once you're married to me...'

He was facing the door and she felt his arms slacken around her. Someone had come in, and she knew at once who it was.

'So sorry,' said the doctor with loud cheerfulness. 'I should have remembered. You really must stay to dinner, Mount, and spend the night too.'

Philip's voice sounded stiff and sullen. 'Thanks— I'd like to stay to dinner; I've already booked at an hotel for the night.'

'Splendid!' Pieter smiled, his eyes icily bright beneath their lids. 'Aap shall show you where you can freshen up presently, but while Phyllida changes we'll have a drink. You're a doctor, are you not? What do you specialise in?'

He barely glanced at Phyllida as he opened the door for her, and when she peeped at him, she could see a mocking little smile on his face.

Her mother and Willy weren't to be found. She

bathed and dressed in the new tunic, did her hair and face with tremendous care and sat down to wait until the very last minute before dinner. The idea of spending even a few minutes with Philip made her feel quite sick. Somehow she would have to get Pieter alone and explain...

She had no chance; when she eventually went downstairs it was to find not only Pieter with his unexpected guest, but her mother, Willy, Pieter's mother and father and Marena, grouped around the log fire, having what appeared to be a high old time over drinks.

Pieter crossed the room to her as she stood, quite taken aback, just inside the door. The nasty little smile was still there, she saw uneasily, and he observed just as nastily: 'A new dress? Very charming—kept for Philip, I suppose.'

'You suppose wrong,' snapped Phyllida very quietly so that no one else could hear. 'It's a new dress, but I bought it for...' She couldn't tell him that she had bought it for his benefit; she closed her mouth firmly and glared at him.

'You didn't know that he was coming?' His soft voice held incredulity.

'Of course I didn't! Pieter—oh, Pieter...'

'Oh, Phylly!' His voice mocked her. 'What will you have to drink?'

Hemlock would have been a good choice, she

thought silently, but aloud she settled for a dry sherry and went to speak to his parents.

Marena was talking to her mother and neither of them looked over-happy. Phyllida smiled emptily at them both and drank her sherry far too quickly, plunging into an animated conversation with Mevrouw van Sittardt and puzzling that lady considerably by answering her questions with a series of random replies, engendered by the sherry and her chaotic thoughts. Out of the corner of her eye she had seen Marena leave her mother and go and stand by Pieter, so close that she was almost in his pocket. No one, she thought bitterly, had warned her that there was to be company for dinner. Which was hardly surprising since the doctor had made lightning telephone calls to his guests at the last minute, intimating that a close friend of Phyllida had arrived to see her and it seemed a good idea to invite a few people to meet him.

His parents had arrived full of curiosity, although to look at their dignified calm, no one would have guessed it; Marena had accepted gleefully, wanting to see Phyllida's close friend. Only Mrs Cresswell had accepted the situation with placid calm, apparently doing nothing about it, merely waiting to see what would happen. She had greeted Philip with well concealed surprise, asked kindly after his wellbeing and engaged Marena in conversation. But now, seeing her daughter looking quite distracted, Mrs Cresswell wandered over to Pieter and Marena, prised her away from him with a ruthless charm which made his blue eyes sparkle with appreciation, and wandered off again, Marena in tow, beckoning to Philip and talking to Willy as she did so.

'Philip, I don't know if Pieter told you, but Marena is an artist—so clever of her, because she's far too pretty to do anything at all, don't you agree?'

Her listeners swallowed this barefaced flattery with no trouble at all; Marena had such a good opinion of herself that she found it not in the least unusual that other people should share it, and as for Philip, he had been staring at her ever since she had entered the room and had longed to talk to her, something his host hadn't seemed to think he might want to do, for he had stationed Philip in front of him so that he had had no more than a glimpse of her from time to time because the doctor's broad person had quite blocked his view.

Mrs Cresswell, standing between them, listened with interest to Philip, usually so staid, letting himself go. The pair of them, she considered, were ideally suited. She sipped her sherry and glanced around the room, to encounter the doctor's hard stare. She returned it with a vague smile and presently he strolled over and invited her to admire the charming view from the window. They stood for a minute admiring the riot of colour outside.

'Mother love is a wonderful thing,' observed the doctor silkily.

'Oh, indeed, yes,' agreed Mrs Cresswell imperturbably, 'it should never be underestimated.'

'How right, Mrs Cresswell. The pity of it is that it is so often called into action when none is required.'

She turned to look at him. 'Interfering?' she asked. 'Now that's something I never do, Pieter.' She gave him one of her vague, sweet smiles. 'What a lovely girl Marena is.'

He didn't answer her, only smiled a little, and a moment later Aap appeared to bid them to dinner.

Later, during a mostly sleepless night, Phyllida reviewed the evening. It had been pure disaster for her; Philip had been placed next to her at table and Pieter had treated her with the politeness of a good host with whom she was only slightly acquainted, and was bent on giving her every opportunity to be alone with Philip. And the awful thing had been that Philip, although he had stuck to her like a leech, could hardly take his eyes off Marena. And when she had tried to get him alone—really alone where they could talk without anyone overhearing them—it had been impossible; Pieter might have contrived in the most ostentatious manner possible that they should be in each other's company, and yet each time she had sneaked off into a quiet corner with Philip, he had materialised like an evil genie and swept them back with the other guests.

Of one thing she was fairly sure—Philip might have come with the intention of asking her to marry him, under the impression that he loved her, but now that he had actually seen her again, he'd gone off her completely. An arrangement which suited her very well if only Pieter hadn't foiled her every chance to tell Philip that. He had even insisted that Philip should call round on the following morning: 'For I'm rather booked up myself,' he had observed urbanely, 'but do consider yourself at home—I hope to be back for lunch, and I'll see you then.' He had added blandly: 'I had arranged to drive Phyllida back, but if she wants to, by all means take her with you.'

And he hadn't even asked her what she had wanted to do! fumed Phyllida, sitting up in bed, choking with temper at the mere memory. 'If he wants to get rid of me, he can,' she cried loudly, 'then he can spend all the time he wants with his beastly Marena. I can't think why he asked me in the first place...'

She had cried then and gone to sleep with puffy red eyes and a pink nose. Her eyes were still puffy when she went down to breakfast, but she hadn't bothered to find her dark glasses; Pieter had said he had a busy morning—at the hospital, she supposed, or Marena, of course.

He was occupied with neither. He was sitting at his breakfast table, chatting pleasantly to Mrs Cresswell and discussing the chances of another fishing trip with Willy. He stood up as Phyllida went in, wished her a cheerful good morning, asked her if she had a cold and added: 'Your eyes are puffy,' before begging her to help herself to anything she fancied.

She didn't fancy anything. She crumbled toast on her plate and drank several cups of coffee and had great difficulty in not throwing a plate at his head when he suggested that she should take a couple of Panadol tablets. 'So that you'll feel up to young Mount's company. Have you decided if you are going back with him, Phylly?'

'If Phylly can bear it, I'd much rather she went back with us,' interposed Mrs Cresswell. 'I really cannot manage by myself,' she explained plaintively. She wasn't going to have to lift a finger, everyone knew that, but Phyllida couldn't agree fast enough, the relief in her voice so obvious that Pieter's mouth twitched and his eyes danced with laughter. But all he said, and that seriously, was:

'Of course—I should have remembered that. Mount will be disappointed.'

'No, he won't,' she snapped, tossing her fringe with a pettish shake of her head. 'I can't think why he came in the first place.'

'My dear Phylly,' his voice was very smooth, 'isn't it obvious why he came?'

She went a fiery red, a dozen furious words on her tongue waiting to be uttered, but she had no chance. Willy said in a matter-of-fact voice: 'He's such a saphead I never thought he'd come after you, Phylly—I mean, he's not really stuck on you, is he?' He added with brotherly candour: 'I daresay he fancied you for a bit—you're not bad to look at, you know.'

This remark was received in silence. The doctor's face was impassive and he had dropped the lids over his eyes so that no one could see their expression. Mrs Cresswell buttered a roll with deliberation before remarking: 'I do not like to curb the young, Willy, but I think that you have rather overreached yourself.' And Phyllida stared at him and then burst out laughing, only half way through the laughter changed to tears. Pieter jumped to his feet, but before he could reach her, she had rushed out of the room.

Pieter sat down again. He said thoughtfully, looking at Mrs Cresswell: 'I can but guess at the reason for that; I can only hope that I have guessed correctly.'

Neither of his two companions answered him; Willy for the obvious reason that it might be better to hold his tongue for a while, and his mother because she could see that the doctor required no answer.

He went away presently and as soon as the Bentley had disappeared Philip arrived in the local taxi and Phyllida came downstairs, greeted him quite cheerfully, explained that she was wearing dark glasses because she had a slight headache, and agreed readily to go for a walk.

She had had a good cry upstairs and time to think. She would have to pretend that she intended to marry Philip because that was what Pieter wanted. They had got a little too friendly, but only through force of circumstances; now he wanted to get back to his Marena. She hadn't been able to understand his bad temper of the previous evening, nor guess at what he had been going to say just before Philip arrived, but it couldn't have been what she had hoped and now she would never know. Besides, he had fairly flung her at Philip... She had stopped thinking about it, otherwise she'd cry again, and had allowed her mind to dwell on their first meeting on Madeira. He had been so easy to like...to love...

She took Philip for a long walk, following the narrow brick roads between the canals, carefully pointing out anything of interest as they went. They had walked for more than half an hour before Philip, abandoning the threadbare theme of the weather upon which she had been harping, said: 'You met this fellow on Madeira, didn't you? I suppose he turned your head and now you fancy you're in love with him, just as I was saying when he interrupted us. He's got a girl anyway, that little beauty who came to dinner.' He added, not unkindly: 'You haven't a chance; you're pretty enough in a nice open-air way, but she's gorgeous.'

Phyllida had stopped so that she might steady her breath and answer him with calm. She would have liked to have screamed at him, but that would have done no good—besides, she had realised something in the last few moments.

She said with an entirely false enthusiasm: 'She's terrific, she's known Pieter van Sittardt for simply ages and I suppose they'll marry sooner or later, but I don't know—I'm not sure if she's in love with him, or he with her.' She added distractedly: 'It's hard to tell, isn't it? Philip, all this time while you thought you were in love with me you weren't, you only thought you were, and now you've discovered you aren't. We get on well, I told you that, but you wouldn't listen, and that's not the same as loving someone. I'm not saying you're in love with Marena, but she excites you as I never did, doesn't she? One day you'll find a girl like her.' She stopped because it had just occurred to her that she would never find a man quite like Pieter, even if she searched for the rest of her life.

'She's wonderful,' said Phillip. 'Why can't I meet a girl like that? Clever and stunning to look at...' He went on awkwardly: 'I say, Phylly, I didn't mean to say that—I mean, you're very pretty and no end of a good companion, but you're right—I came over here intending to ask you to marry me, but now...' He paused and she finished for him:

'And now you've seen me, and you don't want to. Well I don't want to either, so don't waste time on me, Philip; there must be hundreds of girls like Marena—you'll just have to look for them. Why don't you ask her out to dinner? She might have sisters or friends or—or someone...'

They had turned for home once more, not hurrying. 'Well, as a matter of fact I did ask her if she'd have dinner with me. I'll have to go back tomorrow some time, but I can catch the night ferry. She wants to show me her paintings.'

Phyllida stifled a giggle. Marena must have heard that one about men asking girls up to see their etchings—only hers were paintings.

Philip gave her a look of suspicion. 'Why are you giggling?'

'Oh, I'm not,' she denied hastily. 'Philip, don't

get too serious, will you? It wouldn't be fair to cut out Pieter.'

He gave an angry laugh. 'Good lord, I've never met a man more capable of getting his own way! I thought his mother was a bit of a tartar, too.'

'She's a darling,' said Phyllida warmly, instantly up in arms. 'She's a bit—well, large, but she's kind and—and...'

'Oh dear,' his voice mocked her. 'I had no idea you were so keen on her, but I suppose that's natural.'

They could see the house now, through the trees. 'It's a wonderful place he's got here. We had quite a chat yesterday evening. Can't say that I like him, though.'

She thought it very likely that Pieter didn't like him either, but she didn't say so. There was no point in stirring things up; heaven knew that the muddle was bad enough as it was. But at least she and Philip could part finally and on friendly terms. She would go back home, start all over again and forget Pieter and his family and those nice friends of his on Madeira and the brief period of happiness she had had.

'You're not listening,' complained Philip. 'I was telling you about this new job I've applied for.'

Phyllida said she was sorry and gave her full attention to him prosing on about senior registrars' posts and getting a consulting job in a few years' time and his expectations from an elderly grandparent which was going to make his future a decidedly better one. It lasted until they were within a few yards of the garden room, where they paused.

'I've enjoyed this walk,' said Philip in a voice which implied that he hadn't expected to. 'You're an easy person to talk to, Phylly. You don't mind? Us splitting up, I mean.'

Just as though they hadn't split up weeks ago, only he hadn't accepted it then. 'No, I don't mind, Philip, truly I don't—I hope you find a smashing girl and carve a splendid career for yourself, you've started that already.'

'Yes, I haven't done so badly,' he answered her complacently, and put his hands on her shoulders. 'No hard feelings, then?'

He bent to kiss her just as she became aware that the doctor was standing at the open door of the garden room, watching them.

She wriggled free of Philip, muttering that she must tidy herself for lunch and ran indoors, passing Pieter without looking at him, only to be halted by a large hand on her arm. 'So sorry,' he said softly and sikily, 'I always turn up at the wrong moment, don't I?'

She didn't answer, only ducked her head and rushed across the room and out into the hall, to pound up the staircase as though the devil were after her, not stopping until she had reached her room and shut the door. But there was no time in which to have the good howl she ached to have. She did her face, combed her silky hair and went downstairs again, this time at a sedate pace, to find everyone in the drawing room drinking sherry.

Afterwards, she couldn't remember what she had eaten at lunch, nor did she remember a single word she had spoken; presumably she had been quite normal, as no one had stared at her. And after lunch Philip had gone, but only after the doctor had wished him goodbye and then pointedly swept her mother and Willy out into the garden leaving her and Philip together in the hall. It was a pity that there had been no one there to see them shake hands.

There was just one day left now before they were to return home. She spent the night dithering between wishing that Pieter would spend the whole of it at home, and praying fervently that she wouldn't have to see him again until they left. As a consequence she went downstairs to breakfast in the dark glasses again, with a splitting headache and in a frightful temper.

Pieter was at breakfast, although he left within a few minutes of her arrival at the table. During those few minutes he had been his usual placid self, touching only briefly on their journey and reminding them that they would all be dining with his parents that evening. 'And I'm free for a couple of hours after lunch,' he told Willy. 'We might have a last try at catching a pike.' With which he left them, looking so cheerful and normal that she could have thrown something at him.

She mooned about after breakfast, packing for herself and for Willy, strolling round the garden with her mother, and then at her brother's request, walking down to the village for some last-minute trifles he simply had to have. It seemed an age until lunch time and even Lympke's offer to show her the kitchens, semi-basement but still kitchens which a woman might dream of and never have, wasn't sufficient to take her mind off her own troubles. All the same, she admired their size and old-world charm and all the well-concealed modern gadgets. She hoped that when Marena married Pieter, she would appreciate it all. Somehow she doubted that.

When she went into the drawing room, Pieter was already there although her mother and Willy were nowhere to be seen, which seemed strange because she had heard them go down earlier.

'They're down at the lake,' his voice was disarmingly casual. 'The swans are taking the cygnets for their first swim. What will you drink?'

'Sherry, thank you. Have you had a busy morning?'

'Yes, very. And what have you been doing?' He

shot her a glance from under his brows. 'You must miss young Mount.'

She didn't answer that. 'I've been for a walk with Willy and then Lympke took me round the kitchens. They're very—nice,' she finished lamely.

His firm mouth twitched slightly. 'Yes, aren't they? Is there anything you would like to do this afternoon? Shopping? Aap can drive you into Leiden or den Haag.'

They were like two polite strangers and she thought with longing of their easy comradeship. 'No, thank you—I think we've got everything. I expect Mother will want to go round the gardens just once more and I'll go with her, I expect.'

He said carelessly: 'Oh, by all means. Willy and I will be at the lake until tea-time, we don't need to leave for den Haag until seven o'clock.'

He had arranged things very well; she would see almost nothing of him for the rest of the day.

And she didn't, not until the evening, when clad in the jersey tunic, she went downstairs. Pieter and Willy had gone back to the lake after tea and she was reasonably sure that no one would be down yet, as they hadn't returned until almost half past six.

She was wrong. As she reached the hall, Pieter's study door was opened and he came out, dressed for the evening in one of his dark grey, beautifully cut suits; another man entirely from the rubber-booted, sweatered figure which had come hurrying in not half an hour earlier.

He greeted her smilingly and set her teeth on edge with the remark: 'You shouldn't waste that pretty dress on us, you know. What will you drink?'

Phyllida astonished herself and him by asking for whisky, a drink she loathed, but somehow the occasion called for something strong. She sipped it cautiously, trying not to pull a face, and didn't see the amusement in his eyes.

'Was Mount going back today?' asked the doctor casually.

'Yes—on the night ferry. Did you have a busy morning?'

He was kind enough not to remind her that she had asked him that already before lunch, but sketched in his activities at the hospital until Mrs Cresswell and Willy joined them.

The short ride to den Haag was fully taken up with lighthearted talk of the next day's journey, and the other three didn't appear to notice Phyllida's silence. Between her 'yeses' and 'noes' and 'reallys' she was wondering if Marena was going to be there too. Very likely, although it didn't matter any more now. If only she could have had five minutes alone with Pieter while she explained about Philip and herself in the lucid language one always thought of in bed in the dead of night. At least it would clear the

air and they could part friends, but he had given her
no chance to talk—really talk—while they had been
waiting for her mother and Willy, and even if he
had, she thought mournfully, she would quite likely
have burst into tears.

With an effort she stopped thinking about it and
arranged her features into a suitable expression of
pleasure at meeting Pieter's parents again.

The evening lasted for ever, with leisurely drinks
in the magnificent drawing room, preceding an
equally leisurely dinner in the sombre Biedermeier
dining room. Marena wasn't there and her name
wasn't mentioned until very shortly before they left,
when Mevrouw Sittardt asked her son: 'And have
you seen Marena, Pieter? She telephoned here earlier today, thinking you might be with us.'

'I saw her this morning, Mama.' Mother and son
exchanged a long look and Mevrouw van Sittardt
nodded her elegant head, smiling a little. Phyllida,
her ears stretched to hear everything Pieter said, had
heard the brief conversation but hadn't seen the
look. She gazed unseeingly at Pieter's father, telling
her a gently meandering tale about something or
other, not hearing a word of it, wishing she were
anywhere other than where she was; as far away
from Pieter as possible, and wishing at the same
time that she could stay for the rest of her life near
him.

But the doctor appeared to have no such feeling of reluctance at the thought of seeing the last of her. He chatted amiably about her future prospects as he drove home at speed, saw them all safely indoors, bade them a cheerful goodnight and took himself off in the car again.

He got back at two o'clock exactly. Phyllida, who had been lying awake listening for his return, had heard the great Friesian wall clock in the hall boom twice in its majestic voice as Pieter's quiet step mounted the stairs and crossed the corridor to his own room.

Of course he had been with Marena. She stayed awake for another two hours, her imagination running riot, until sheer exhaustion sent her finally to sleep.

CHAPTER NINE

THE RETURN TO England went smoothly. To Phyllida, sitting in the back of the Bentley with her mother, it went far too quickly too. Pieter had hardly spoken to her beyond polite enquiries as to her comfort, observations upon the weather and the remark that she looked tired. It wasn't until they were speeding in the direction of Shaftesbury with the greater part of their journey behind them that she found herself sitting beside him. She wasn't sure how this had happened; they had stopped because Willy had been thirsty and she had found herself propelled gently into the front seat without being able to do much about it. She sat silent, turning just a little sideways, so that she could watch his large capable hands on the wheel. They had covered quite a few miles before he spoke. 'Will you be seeing young Mount?'

'No.' She added hastily: 'Well, not straight away.' It would never do for him to discover that she and Philip, although they had parted friends, were unlikely to meet again.

The doctor grunted. 'It seems a long time since we first met.'

She was breathless. 'Yes, ages.'

'The de Meesters asked after you in their last letter—they would like you to visit them again.'

'That's very kind of them, but I don't suppose I shall ever go back to Madeira.'

'What's happened to us, Phylly?' he asked softly. 'Or rather, what's happened to you?'

It was difficult to get the words out. 'Me? Nothing—what should have happened? I've had a lovely holiday and now I've got to find a job.' She added for good measure: 'I can hardly wait!'

His voice was casual. 'And Philip—he won't mind you working?'

'It's no busi... He won't mind in the least.'

He slid the car past a coach load of tourists. 'I must confess I'm puzzled, Phylly—I understood you to say that you weren't going to marry young Mount. But of course when he turned up unexpectedly like that, you probably realised that you'd made a mistake.'

She muttered something or other, longing to tell him just how she felt, wondering what he would say if she told him that she loved him to distraction. He would be very nice about it, but it was hardly likely that it would alter his feelings for Marena. She sighed, a sad little sound which caused him to glance at her quickly and then again, a little smile lifting the corners of his mouth. When he spoke he sounded very matter-of-fact. 'We shan't be long now—half an hour, I would think.'

Home looked lovely as the car swooped gently down the hill and up the other side, and when they stopped before the door there was Beryl to welcome them and a moment later Doctor Cresswell. Everyone talked at once, unloading luggage, urging the travellers to go indoors, offering refreshment. They all surged into the sitting room finally, still talking and laughing, and Phyllida, watching her family clustered round Pieter, suddenly couldn't bear it any longer. He would be gone soon; she had heard him say only a moment ago that although he had hoped to spend the night with them, he had discovered that it wouldn't be possible after all. She slid out of the room and into the kitchen, where the kettle was boiling its head off beside the waiting teapot. She made the tea, put on the lid and then stood looking at it, willing herself not to cry. She didn't hear Pieter come in and it wasn't until he spoke that she whisked round to face him.

'Well, I must be on my way, Phylly.' He smiled at her and her heart rocked. 'I had hoped...' he paused and sighed gustily. She felt his hands on her shoulders and his light kiss on her cheek.

'I'm not a great lover of poetry,' he told her, 'but there's a verse by John Clare which seems appropriate to the occasion; it goes something like this:

''Last April Fair, when I got bold with beer—I loved her long before, but had a fear to speak.'' I don't know how it ends, but I hope he was luckier than I.'

He had gone as quietly as he had come, out of the room, into the hall, out of the house. Out of her life.

She stood exactly as he had left her for the space of several seconds while the verse rang in her ears. Suddenly she gave a small scream, galloped out of the room in her turn and flung herself at the front door which she banged behind her, to slide to a shaky halt by the Bentley.

Pieter was behind the wheel and the engine was ticking over nicely.

'Pieter—Pieter, don't go. You can't go!' Her voice rose to a wail. 'Can't you see, it's not me and Philip—you thought it was, didn't you? and I pretended it was because I thought it was you and Marena, but it's not, it's you and me, Pieter. Pieter darling!'

He switched off the engine, got out of the car unhurriedly and opened his arms. They were gentle and strong around her, crushing her to his great chest so that it was hard for her to breathe.

'My own dear darling, you've got it right at last.' He smiled down at her and her heart, already doing overtime, leapt into her throat so that she couldn't speak. Not that it mattered. He bent his head and kissed her, soundly and at length, and she kissed him back.

'My darling girl, I love you,' said Pieter in the kind of voice which left her in no doubt about it. And Mrs Cresswell, happening to glance out of her bedroom window at that moment, had no doubts either. She hurried downstairs to tell her husband, talking to herself as she went. 'I thought they never would—at least, Pieter knew, but Phylly—dear child, so dense sometimes!' Her thoughts kept pace with her hurrying feet. 'I shall wear one of those large flowery hats—the bride's mother always does…' She broke off to say to Willy, coming upstairs towards her: 'Wash your hands, dear. I think Pieter and Phylly have just got engaged.'

'Oh, good—now I can go and stay with them and fish. Pieter will like that.'

It was hardly the moment in which to tell the boy that his future brother-in-law might not share his enthusiasm, at least not for the first few months. She said: 'Yes, dear, won't that be nice? Don't forget your hands,' and hurried on down to the study.

Phyllida, being kissed again, found the breath to mutter: 'I thought you were in love with Marena. Oh, Pieter, I'm crazy about you,' and then: 'You were going away.'

She felt his chest heave with laughter. 'No, my

dearest girl, I wasn't going away. I thought that if I came and sat in the car you might think that I was...'

She stared at him and then began to laugh. 'Pieter, oh, Pieter!' and then seriously: 'You won't do it again, will you?'

'Leave you? No, my darling, I'll never do that.'

They didn't notice when the milkman stopped his float alongside the Bentley; they didn't notice as he squeezed past them, nor did they hear his cheerful good morning. He left his bottle on the doorstep and wriggled past them once more.

'All I can say is,' said the milkman to no one in particular, 'it's a very good morning for some of us, and that's a fact.'

Harlequin Romance®

Delightful

Affectionate

Romantic

Emotional

Tender

Original

Daring

Riveting

Enchanting

Adventurous

Moving

Harlequin Romance—the
series that has it all!

HROM-G

HARLEQUIN PRESENTS®

The world's bestselling romance series...
The series that brings you your favorite authors,
month after month:

Helen Bianchin...Emma Darcy
Lynne Graham...Penny Jordan
Miranda Lee...Sandra Morton
Anne Mather...Carole Mortimer
Susan Napier...Michelle Reid

and many more uniquely talented authors!

Wealthy, powerful, gorgeous men...
Women who have feelings just like your own...
The stories you love, set in exotic, glamorous locations...

HARLEQUIN PRESENTS,
Seduction and passion guaranteed!

Visit us at www.eHarlequin.com

HPGEN00

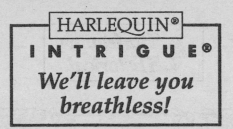

Harlequin® Historical

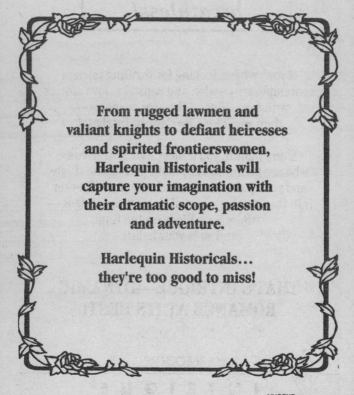

From rugged lawmen and
valiant knights to defiant heiresses
and spirited frontierswomen,
Harlequin Historicals will
capture your imagination with
their dramatic scope, passion
and adventure.

Harlequin Historicals…
they're too good to miss!

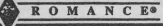

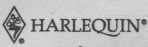